Through the Pale Door

THROUGH *the* PALE DOOR

a novel

Brian Ray

HUB CITY WRITERS PROJECT

First printing, July 2009
Printed in China

Edited by C. Michael Curtis
Proofreaders: Betsy Teter, Susanna Brailsford, Sara June Goldstein,
and Teresa J. Wallace
Cover and text design by Emily Smith
Cover photograph © Coco Amardeil / Zefa / Corbis

The South Carolina First Novel Prize is a collaboration among the
South Carolina Arts Commission, the South Carolina State Library, the
Humanities Council SC, and the Hub City Writers Project. The inaugural
contest was judged by distinguished novelist Percival Everett.

Library of Congress Cataloging-in-Publication Data

Ray, Brian, 1982-
Through the pale door / Brian Ray.
p. cm.
ISBN 978-1-891885-66-2
1. Teenage girls--Fiction. 2. Artists--Fiction. 3. Children of the mentally
ill--Fiction. 4. Mothers--Death--Fiction. 5. Bereavement--Psychological
aspects--Fiction. 6. Fathers and daughters--Fiction. 7. Psychological fiction.
I. Title.
PS3618.A9822T48 2009
813'.6--dc22
2009001291

09   10   11   12   13   C   5   4   3   2   1

Hub City Writers Project
Post Office Box 8421
Spartanburg, SC 29305
864.577.9349 • fax 864.577.0188
www.hubcity.org

For my family, mentors, and friends

And travellers, now, within that valley,
    Through the red-litten windows see
Vast forms, that move fantastically
    To a discordant melody;
While, like a ghastly rapid river,
    Through the pale door
A hideous throng rush out forever
    And laugh—but smile no more.

— Edgar Allen Poe, "The Haunted Palace"

1

M Y DAD TALKED ME INTO WORKING AT THE MILL that summer, my last before college. A job in the steel industry paid
three times what I made as a waitress downtown, so I was sold on
the idea after two or three phone calls. All year I'd never come home
from the diner with more than a sneeze of bills and loose change,
plus some fratty's phone number crayoned across the back of an
orphaned receipt. All of my clothes smelled like two in the morning—spilt beer, burnt coffee, secondhand smoke. I'd often reminded
myself that all great artists started somewhere. A job at my dad's
mill, at least, promised a better start than what I had so far. When
May arrived and school ended, one branch on the oleander in my
mom's yard "bloomed" for a day and then fell onto the driveway, like
a bride's severed arm. My mom saw it happen and smiled. Figures.
Growing up in Alabama, she used to drown cats in the river.

"You could never kill those fuckers," she once told me. "Hold
them with a stick for three minutes, five, eight, water gushing over
them. Their heads would pop right up as soon as you let go, and off
they scampered. Wish I had that kind of resilience. Anyway, killing
them wasn't my idea. My mom told me to do it. Cats spread disease,
she said. They were a total plague."

My last Saturday morning in Marietta, Georgia, the mountains stood in the middle of my window as usual, bored and tired of being covered with trees. My high school graduation gown swayed in the closet. It caught some wind from the open window and ballooned out, a kind of momentary sail. I arose to spend a few minutes in the shower and then, deciding to skip the day's ceremony altogether, I packed my clothes and art supplies into the backseat and mapped the three-hour drive to Columbia, South Carolina, where my dad had moved after my parents divorced a year earlier. Hoping to leave without a prolonged goodbye, I didn't wake my mom.

I should have.

In a way, I didn't have to. Her paintings did plenty of talking for both of us. She'd hung them in the upstairs hallway, living room, den, kitchen, everywhere. Someone died in every single one—victims of various mill accidents. Men drowned in bowls of hot metal. They dangled from construction cranes by nooses made of power cables. Their crumpled bodies accordioned out of twelve-ton stacks of rebar. In her recent masterpieces, the victims resembled my dad. They were a kind of voodoo, or maybe just wishful thinking. My mom once said that Picasso never used the switchblade of cubism to draw the people he loved. But there my dad lies, in a work entitled *No. 7*, limp on the floor of an overstocked warehouse, his body peeled like an orange.

Was I next?

Even if I didn't die in my mom's paintings, the threats of a steel plant were real. My dad had promised me I'd be safe. "Don't worry, Sarah. Only the dropouts have to work in the melt shop, and that's the most dangerous place," he'd said over the phone. "You'll probably assist the receptionist in various ways."

"That's thoughtful of you," I said.

"I know."

Every time we talked long distance, I imagined his attention aimed at a calculator or some broken gadget he'd pried open. My dad never quite looked me in the eye. Even when he did, he seemed to be watching some part of the eye, a slash of black in the green iris or a red scrawl on the white. I didn't mind those parts of the eye, the blood vessels. They reminded me of someone testing out a pen. Still, I tried to make the people on the other end of my conversations feel important. My dad somehow failed.

"You'll be safe," he'd said, to finally reassure me. "I'll bet you won't even lose a finger."

MY MOM HAD SKETCHED ME the afternoon I first told her about working at the mill. She'd smiled acidly from her side of the kitchen table, unwilling to share my enthusiasm. "You're eighteen, and your dad wants you to start turning a profit. That's all. Now, raise your head. Keep your hands still. And stop blinking."

Like a good model, I tried to speak without moving my lips. "Dad says it's worth the money."

"Let me tell you about your dad and money." My mom slashed at her sketchbook. "Right before he was baptized, the preacher held out a Bible and a twenty dollar bill. The preacher told him to pick one. He picked the twenty."

"Mom, you haven't been to church in twenty years. Do you really care?"

She glared at her sketch, as if my image had just contradicted her. "Your dad says he already had a Bible, and that's why. But he doesn't get it. The whole thing wasn't about God. Stop blinking, Sarah. It was about greed. We've argued for years."

"Don't I know that already? You guys argued all the time."

"We always argued privately, in the bathroom or the garage, never in front of you."

"We're arguing about arguing."

"You started."

"About the whole Bible thing, isn't he also standing up for what he wants? If my dad wanted the twenty, then he did the right thing. Besides, how can I not blink? You've been painting for thirty years, and you've never complained about blinking."

"The general act of blinking doesn't bother me. It's you blinking, here and now. So, stop. I don't know why. Today, your blinking bothers me. End of story."

"Would've been worse to take the Bible if he didn't want it," I said.

"Go on," she said, trying to hold her mug and charcoal in the same hand. "I'm listening."

"Good," I said. "The real issue is conformity. Taking the Bible, he would've been doing what everybody wanted him to."

"Don't give him that much credit," she said. "What other people want has never, in my opinion, factored into your dad's thoughts." My mom suddenly slammed her sketch book on the table. "For God's sake, Sarah, stop blinking. Some people can stare without blinking for up to an hour. You can stop blinking for twenty minutes, can't you? It's not an unreasonable demand. So many people ask you to do things. I'm simply asking you *not* to do something."

That's why my dad had left, I guessed. His wants trumped our needs. The decision had nothing to do with his promotion or the fact that my mom was insane, like an unwound ball of yarn, tangled and sprawling, dangerous. She'd tried to kill him once, and me. Things were better lately, though the social services woman came once or even twice a month. In South Carolina you can decide at age sixteen which parent you want to stay with, just like you can marry any man you please. My dad had asked me to stay here and keep my mom's yarn clumped together.

So that Saturday morning I simply packed my car and drove straight to the plant. Three hours placed me on a shredded road that carved across an obstacle course of train tracks and then plunged into the woods. How a steel mill could hide out here in this forest baffled me. Spanish moss hung so low from the oaks it nearly brushed the top of my car. I could barely see beyond the next bend in the road until, a mile or two down, the wilderness opened up and factory buildings began to peek out from the treetops. The scene reminded me of the books where explorers stumble onto a city of ruins in some lush jungle.

Something screamed out from the distant steel plant, a whistle or siren, and I imagined someone was being sacrificed. My mom had done a series of paintings on that theme. She'd drawn my dad and some of his mill friends, their hardhats transformed into ceremonial headdresses, carving open young girls and boys and tugging out their guts. I'd begged her to make me a sacrifice. She never did.

The road led to a wide concrete parking lot, half-filled with dingy pickup trucks and trailers. I parked and climbed out of my car. The noise I encountered was thick and grainy, so loud it was like silence. My dad wasn't waiting up front like he'd said. But he'd left a uniform, hard hat, and a pair of boots with the security guard. I tugged on the boots. They had thick steel toes and an oversized steel tongue that covered the entire top of each foot. I practiced walking in them. Then the guard handed me a bright orange jacket and some safety glasses and earplugs. The jacket was stiff, made from flame retardant fabric. The guard laughed and said that someone could hold a torch to me now and I wouldn't catch fire.

"What if someone came after me with a flame thrower?" I said.

"Then that wouldn't be an accident," he said. "So, you ever see a man's lighter burst into flames in his pocket?"

"No, do I want to?"

"We've got some footage in a safety video. It's pretty cool to watch."

Waiting for my dad, I watched the mill through a fence, like someone at a zoo. A trio of trucks rolled to a stop at the back of the melt shop, where they dumped scrap into heaps. Giant claws descended onto the heaps, grabbed handfuls of the scrap, and dropped them. The scrap clattered into the furnace.

I remembered tours my dad had given when I was six or seven. Generally, I knew how the plant operated. Inside the melt shop, a furnace charged 80,000 volts of electricity through the scrap, turning it into neon-red magma. The magma poured into a large metal bowl called a ladle, which emptied into a castor, which then spewed the magma into rectangular molds, forming billets. The billets cooled as they slid out of the melt shop in long crimson bars. The billets were then hefted up by a magnetic crane and carried to the rolling mill, which crafted them into one of four products: rebar, flats, angles, and channels. The various products wound up in everything from roofs to bridges.

I found a note in my jacket pocket from my dad. He apologized for the long wait, and told me that if he hadn't arrived yet that I should wait outside the "old" rolling mill.

This was informative.

After all, most of the buildings here looked old—worn and scarred by a succession of decades. To find my desired location, I had to follow the pointing fingers of helpful passersby. At a certain point I crossed a thin metallic bridge that cut between the melt shop and billet yard. As I crossed the bridge, I glanced halfway up the melt shop's façade and saw something truly remarkable for a steel mill. A mural, which kicked open my eyes like rusty doors. I hadn't expected to see visual art out here.

The mural, the length of my arm span, portrayed a skeleton giving birth to a baby skeleton the size of my palm. Both skeletons were deep black against a wall of red, as if someone had welded them together from strips of nighttime and held them over a fire. My mom must've painted this, I thought, however unlikely. The deep, sharp contours and curved diagonal lines resembled those in her work, but somebody else must have done it. My mom couldn't have come to Columbia without telling me.

Another similarity lay in my own reaction. My stomach suddenly felt heavy and began to bulge. I felt the stab of pregnancy, as if a razor-sharp fetus were cutting into the inside wall of my womb. If this mural had played a song, it would've played the second part to Stravinsky's *Rite of Spring*, "Dances of the Young Girls and Boys."

I stopped a worker as his feet clanked across the metal bridge and asked him if he knew who'd painted these brutal corpses.

The man had a mustache, like my dad, which he flattened with a finger as he eyed me through dark sunglasses. "Nobody knows who does them."

"Them, as in more than one?"

The man's head twisted left, and he pointed toward an alley. Bright red steel trickled along a rough, ashy ground. Along the alley walls, the mystery muralist had painted a dozen muscular gods hammering crimson hot swords. My mom had never painted anything this epic. I felt thrown backward in time five-thousand years. I imagined the artist who'd painted these works to be a man with thick vines for arms, carrying a paintbrush that weighed a hundred pounds. I swooned.

"How can nobody know?" I asked the man in sunglasses.

He spread gravel with his foot, shrugging. "These paintings just kind of show up. Nobody hires nobody to come out here."

"He does this for free?"

"If you ask me, more than one got to be behind them things. Only a real lunatic would spend that much of his free time out here, though I happen to think they brighten up the place some. Others ain't too fond. Plus, if whoever don't work here, they're liable to injure themselves and cost us some big bucaroonies." The man glanced at his watch and tipped his hard hat. "Well, nice talking to you, little miss. But now I got to get back to work."

Maybe my dad had hired someone to paint the murals, I thought. Or maybe one of my mom's students had driven here out of homage. Explanations were endless, but therefore useless. I walked on, trying to pretend I hadn't noticed anything.

When I reached the old mill, the place was overrun with grease-coated men in jumpsuits. I navigated the crowd, looking for my dad, but was greeted only by wave upon wave of dark, sooty grins.

One of the plant electricians told me that my dad had gone out to lunch with some important clients. I could return to the front gate or, if I wanted, I could sit here and watch them dissect the old rolling mill. "Your dad masterminded this project. Last May he showed everybody how we'd double production by building a new mill. We finished construction a couple weeks ago, and he was right. We're already seeing a rise in profits. So now we're gutting this old hunk of crap, saving parts we can sell off."

"Makes sense," I said. "Doesn't my dad mastermind everything?"

The electrician smiled. Or I thought he did. I couldn't quite tell, really. Grime and soot had camouflaged his lips. "I reckon he does."

"By the way," I said. "Do you happen to have any idea who's been painting all of these murals?

"Miss, if you was to figure out that mystery, well, you'd have a leg up on most folks." He waved goodbye and rejoined the indistinguishable painted faces. I searched for a safe place to perch. But, no matter where I stood, I was always in the way. Men with wrenches and power tools and chainsaws kept telling me where I'd be safer before they pushed past me, grumbling blue-collar language.

The old rolling mill looked to be under siege. In addition to the hoards coming and going on foot, more workers hung off an outer wall, cutting through pipes and ducts with blow torches. The old mill's insides glowed like thunderheads full of lightning. Sitting down, I pulled a receipt from my pocket and sketched the scene until someone told me I'd best not look straight at the blow torches, unless I wanted to go blind.

"Hey," shouted one man, "we're about to park a dumpster right where you be sitting. Better get out the way."

When the man had guided me to a safe spot, he touched his finger on his chin. The finger sponged off a patch of grime, leaving a white splotch of clean skin. "Hmm, we got to find some place to put the man-lift, too. I figure it'll have to go right here."

I asked, "What's a man-lift?"

He pointed down the walkway at a machine on wheels that reminded me of a giraffe. At the head of the machine's long neck was a platform with yet another man on top, who controlled the vehicle with switches and levers. The man-lift crawled forward. I walked backward, trying to stay out of everyone's way, until something bleeped at me.

I had stepped inadvertently into the billet yard. An overhead crane's emergency lights strobed as the operator leaned out of the window. "Hey, watch out now."

At first, I overlooked the dull gray swirls on the old mill's starboard side. This factory towered over the landscape, and so I had to walk backward fifty feet to follow the dynamic paths of these swirls to discern their cumulative image. Once I gained perspective, I became entranced in these spirals. They were a pair of eyes, enormous, like the ones in Fitzgerald's novel. But I guessed they didn't symbolize God. No, something darker peered into me.

"Who are you?" I whispered.

After I'd given up on finding my dad, or a safe place to wait for him, I went for a long walk around the plant, hoping to pass the time.

I'd forgotten how much space steel needed. A quarter of a mile placed me before the new rolling mill, a long rectangular block with a golden sheen to the surface. Another quarter of a mile placed me in the vast plains of the storage yards. Rusted stacks of rebar and piles of scrap stank like elephants. I couldn't hide from the sun, which turned gravel into hot coals. A dirt devil spun to life there and spiraled up a hundred feet, sucking paper bags and Coke cans into its brown cloud.

The devil skipped and swept across the desert of the storage yard. I almost expected the thing to leave all the litter in a neat pile when it was done. My dad had told stories about dirt devils. They chased forklifts around the plant. They were harmless, but they struck fear and awe into a small crowd of crane operators and welders that gathered to pay homage to weather.

I walked on, my patience wearing thin. The sun invaded me like a virus. I began to feel dizzy from the heat. So I made my way back to main gate, which was further than I thought. If my first day proceeded this way, I would shrivel and die. My soul would stay here and wander about, searching warehouses and storage yards. Time would erode the old mill and the new mill alike, and I would remain in this terrible state of waiting for someone to show up.

My dad made quite the entrance, when he finally appeared. Just when my thoughts had begun to drift, a buzz grew out of the general noise of the mill. At first I thought it was a bee or a wasp hovering at the backside of my ear, trying to whisper some important information. The longer I listened, the louder it got, splitting off from the general racket to become its own sound. The waves finally crystallized into the thumping of a helicopter. The copter passed over the mill, descending behind the shipping warehouse. Intuition told me to head that way. When I got to the landing site, I saw my dad strapped into the copter's bubble-shaped head. He lifted the flight helmet off and reached into the back for his hardhat.

Clothes flapping under the blades, I folded my hands at my back and prepared for a comatose greeting. I'd been trained not to expect hugs. A simple hello always did best, even after long absences. "How've you been?" I said, when he nodded in my direction.

"Production record this week." His fingers fondled his front pocket for a cigarette. "Can't do better than that. Let's go over to the office."

He paced off, and I struggled to keep up in my boots. "Mom seems better than ever now that she's on the new stuff. I forget what it's called. It's been almost a year now, and no breakdowns."

"Good," he said, smoke escaping from the side of his mouth. Chugging forward, he looked a bit like a train. "In a way, I'd hope so. We pay enough for it. The new stuff's double what they charge for anything else." A gust of ash hit me in the face. "Oh, well. Cheaper than the alternative."

He meant the asylum. I knew that wasn't the correct term. You were supposed to say clinic or hospital, but after eight years of frequent visits that's how I'd come to see the place. My mom had circled in and out of there like a first grader who's just discovered a department store's revolving doors.

Our conversation took us around the east side of the new rolling mill and through the shipping warehouse, down a driveway crammed with sixteen-wheelers and criss-crossed by overhead cranes. We eventually reached a concrete office block, painted tan, with two offices and a break room on one side and a staircase on the other that climbed up to his throne room. "I didn't know you were a pilot," I said. "You didn't say anything about that over the phone."

"I've always known how to fly. So, did you wait around all day?"

I nodded.

He pulled open the door and led us down a hall that opened into other offices for assistants and managers. "When we punch you into the system, I'll add eight hours to your payroll time."

I nodded again. We stopped outside his door. With a jagged key, he tore open the day's mail left in his hanging mailbox.

Then he looked at me, for the first time in a year.

"Those clothes are no good for a steel mill." He shook his head. "Look at how dusty you've gotten. Come on, I'll take the rest of the day off."

"The day's over, practically."

"Not for the boss. I used to head home around four or five, but since the promotion I've been grabbing a late lunch around two. I'll come back and stay until about nine. Anyway, we need to buy you some work clothes to wear under that jacket."

I rolled my eyes, and as I did, I noticed more artwork on a ceiling tile. A young man smiled down at me, tipping his hard hat. As my dad straightened the collar of his jacket and made toward the door, I snagged his sleeve. "Hey, do you have any idea who's the one behind these paintings?" I pointed his attention to the tile.

My dad frowned through his mustache. "Not a clue, though I'll make a note to replace that tile."

"Oh, wait. Can I have the tile?'

"As you please."

I carried the picture under my arm.

In the car, on our way to the thrift shop, I tried to come up with something interesting to say about myself while he talked about work. Screw ups, accidents, names of co-workers I'd heard about for a year but never met. I didn't like blathering about school or my job or art around my dad, mostly because his face always blanked, and he started playing with the radio. But after ten minutes of highway, an awkward silence was suffocating us. Perhaps I had something worthy in my head.

"So this funny thing happened at the diner my last night," I said. I rubbed my hands on my legs, watching his hand go for the dial. What the hell, I thought. Just talk. "A guy in a top hat and a beard came in drunk as sin and tried to recite the Gettysburg Address. Then he changed into a Union Army outfit and started throwing up." Eventually we found out he was a reenactor from out of town who'd gotten lost on his way to Stone Mountain and decided, instead, to drink himself to sleep.

I finished with a triumphant nod of the head and glanced at the driver's seat.

"We just might get lucky on a parking spot," my dad said. "Keep an eye out on your side."

The radio's volume had steadily risen over the course of the story. We made a truce, to agree I hadn't said anything.

The front door of the thrift shop was like a steel trap. I pried it open and held it for my dad, remembering our last shopping trip about a year ago, right around the time he was leaving for Columbia. He wanted my advice on suitcases. At Sears, our first stop, he'd forgotten to hold the door and it bopped me in the head. Onlookers' responses had ranged from gasp to chuckle. It was one of many moments when he'd "forgotten you were coming with me." Of course, I've been told I'm a little clumsy and absent-minded when I come or go.

He led me on a scavenger hunt through bargain bins at the Salvation Army, which sold the best moth-drilled jeans and shirts you could buy for a dollar. Following my dad through a landfill of old children's shoes, I asked about my specific job and responsibilities, which had remained vague. I asked if I'd be working with computers, and he told me those jobs had all gone to boys. I told him I wasn't thrilled with manual labor, but he assured me, "If you want to be an artist, Sarah, then you'd better get used to shitty jobs. Now, what do you think of these pants?"

"They're camouflage," I said. "It's a little flashy."

"They'll help you fit in," he said. "Other workers wear camouflage."

"It just isn't me. They don't match any clothes I own."

"Don't women wear colors that match their eyes?" he said, squinting at me as he rubbed his chin. "You have camouflage eyes."

As an ex-colonel, my dad tried to weave military vocabulary into my life any time he could. This was the first time he'd compared my eyes to camouflage, but he'd described them more than once like the jungles of Vietnam. Shaking my head, I folded the camouflage pants up, dropped them back into the bargain bin, and waited for a reaction. But he'd abandoned my work-clothes quest all together to check out the combat boots, army hats, mesh vests, Kevlar helmets, and a rack of coffee-stained army jackets. While he shopped for his past, I loaded down my shoulders with generic jeans and shirts, enough for a week of grease.

My dad paid cash for my new wardrobe, but he bought nothing for himself.

On our way out he charged through the door. I bolted forward to catch up. The door snapped back before I could get through, punching me in the forehead. The door was a heavy metal hatch. I felt like my skull had been cracked. My hand flew to my face and I stumbled back into a coat rack, then into a chair.

"Good Lord, Jeff," someone yelled. "Been telling you to fix that damn door."

A small crowd gathered as I moaned, holding my head as if it might fall apart.

The shadow of my dad fell across me. I couldn't look up or open my eyes. "Sorry," he said. "I forgot you were here."

Something slid into my hand, something crisp, paper. Ah, money. When my eyes opened he was gone, and three old ladies were helping me to my feet. I studied the bill. A fifty. I wonder how much a genuine fracture would've been worth.

At his house, we waited an hour for the lasagna to cook through the center. I fiddled with the tassel of my graduation cap and watched him admire the steel samples he'd carried home from work. My dad didn't just make steel. He used it to decorate the house. Back in Marietta my mom had waged cold wars against him over the living room. Sometimes she filled entire crates with hunks of melted alloys that she left out for the garbage men, who must've thought our family was disposing of a giant meteorite a few hunks at a time.

My dad's fingers cradled each steel circle as he held it up to the kitchen chandelier and licked it and polished the surface to a glow before placing it in a box. From my chair, the samples looked like an arrangement of shotgun shells.

He placed the box in a corner and flipped open his laptop to browse the steel mill's production page. "Think I'll log in and see how many tons we've shipped since I left. By the way, I had a little time to spruce up the new place." He motioned to the living room then, where I saw my portrait of him propped against the fireplace. Above it loomed an array of metals he'd somehow fastened to the wall.

I admired my portrait of him, in which he stood against a clouded sky with the steel mill in the background, hard-hatted and leaning against a forklift, hands in his pockets.

"Where do you plan to hang that?" I said.

He followed my eyes to the portrait, fingers still tapping away at his laptop. "Maybe in your room."

"What about the mugs?" I said. In order to graduate I'd drawn sixteen black and white charcoals of the same table, nothing on it except a coffee mug and a pitcher. "Did you put them upstairs?"

"Yes, they're in the attic for now."

I huffed. All of that work, now at rest with spiders and forgotten stuffed animals and five boxes of outdated chemical engineering manuals and calculus workbooks from my dad's days in college. My art teacher had made me memorize the human skeleton for a fall semester project. When I decided to draw mugs, he'd made me learn the history of ceramics. I'd drawn hundreds of cups of coffee before Mr. Anjalu had even let me begin the final sixteen drawings. Near the end of the project I'd considered giving up caffeine.

My dad continued to read inventory lists on his computer, stroking a hunk of metal that resembled a crumpled sheet of paper in shape. "Guess I'll start learning the lay of the land," I said, then left the table and gave myself a tour of the house.

His metal collection included copper, cadmium, iron, gold, silver, platinum, chrome, aluminum, and a solar system of other metals whose names I couldn't pronounce. In various spots hung photographs of Bethlehem Steel from the 1930s and present day. Now the plant was abandoned, a conglomeration of buildings as big as airport hangars—nothing inside them but exposed beams.

Before going to bed my dad showed me the way to the lifeless cube that would serve as my room for the next two months. No curtains. No furniture. Not even pictures of Bethlehem Steel's empty buildings. Just a hardwood floor and barren walls. I circled through the room and asked him where I would sleep.

He cocked his head and said that was a good question.

As I waited for an answer, he brought out a stack of quilts from the attic and made a nest in one corner with pillows and throw cushions. We parted in the hallway. I beat out the covers and checked for spider eggs and dead bugs, then lay down and listened to my dad as he fell asleep watching old war documentaries.

I wanted to kick myself now. The couple of artists I knew had at least landed gigs at summer camps, teaching kids how to smear primary colors on cardboard paper. Mr. Anjalu had offered me a summer job as his nude model and personal assistant. When I'd declined, he offered the position to my mom, who said I was a fool for passing up the chance. The air conditioner cut on, filling my ears with a pulsating hum. I thought about my mom and what she must've been doing now, back in Marietta. Smoking a cigarette before her easel, most likely, wishing for someone to bug. My mom had a habit of doing that. For the past year, she'd kept me up past midnight many nights, making me listen to her theories on art. In fact, she often liked to stand behind me in the afternoons and watch me draw. "Try a softer pencil," she'd say, or "that shadow is way too deep." The more I remembered, the less I regretted my decision. Out here, at least, I'd be able to draw in peace.

2

M Y SECOND DAY AT WORK, I stepped into the steel trap of romance. The boy's name was Edgewood, and things began between us after my dad spent an hour on the phone in an attempt to find me a specific job. Nobody wanted a girl to help with anything. The receptionists would not even let me answer the phone. They explained that a teenager, no matter how polite, should never be the first to greet a potential customer. Better to have a man, or the voice of a woman roughened by years in a man's world. My dad agreed. Finally, he handed me a broom and told me to find places that needed sweeping.

Near lunchtime, I'd collapsed onto the sun-scorched metal staircase of some concrete building, letting the red steel hypnotize me as it slid out of the melt shop. Then a guy about my age drove up in a forklift the size of a bad dream. He parked just within the shade of the billet yard and doused his tongue with the last few ounces of water from a plastic canteen. His head turned, and I realized that each of us was looking at the other. Maybe he was a mirage, or to him maybe I was the mirage.

He started his forklift and hummed off, leaving a tail of dust in the air.

Several minutes later, he returned with an extra canteen. He took a seat on the stairs beside me and laid the canteen between us.

He was only a little taller than me, slim and neat looking, if you didn't count the grease on his neck. His face was pleasant, graced by a flat forehead and nice sturdy jaw. He had thick dark eyebrows, and a few sweaty black locks of hair had escaped his hardhat. I smiled, trying not to let him see me looking. I caught myself twirling my hair, and so did he. Embarrassed, I slapped my hands together in my lap. He opened his own canteen and poured water down his throat. Essentially, he was a beautiful human being. I could've watched him drink water for the rest of the afternoon.

He patted the extra canteen he'd brought.

"Is that for me?" I said.

"No, just in case I finish this one."

"Oh, all right." I sighed, still looking at him.

"I was just kidding," he said. "I brought the canteen for you."

I held the canteen against my sternum, by its strap, as if he'd just given me a diamond necklace. "Really, for me?"

He nodded.

"Thank you," I said. "I'm pretty thirsty."

"Yeah, that happens," he said. "So what's your job?"

"Honestly, I'm not sure yet."

"You want to cool off for a bit?" he asked. "Believe it or not, my forklift's got air conditioning."

We climbed into his forklift, exchanging nervous smiles. It relieved me to assume this boy handled courtship as strangely as I did. He opened my door, as if we were already on a date.

The cool air helped me regain my senses. He didn't introduce himself, but his hard hat did. When he threw it in the floorboard at my feet, I picked it up and brailed his name plate with my thumb.

"Edgewood," I said. "Where'd you get that name?"

"It's a street in my hometown," he said. He made a u-turn, and we charged off toward a strip of warehouses, all of which had been tunneled through so vehicles could pass in and out.

"Edgewood," I repeated. "Your parents named you after a street, huh? What's your real name?"

"Maybe I'll tell you later."

I took off my hardhat and safety glasses, nestling them in my lap, then shook out my hair.

"Wow," he said. "You've got a lot of hair."

"Sorry," I said.

"No, I like your hair."

"Really?" I touched the back of my head.

"A few women work out here," Edgewood continued, "and most of them cut their hair short, given the heat and everything. How'd you fit all of that hair into your hard hat?"

"They gave me an extra-large, I guess."

We talked while he went about his job. He did well, holding up conversation while maneuvering this giant elephant of a machine. He stacked bundles of steaming steel into rectangles. But the ride was rough. His foot shook off and back onto the gas, making me lurch forward. "Watch out," he said. "No seatbelts on the passenger side."

Despite air conditioning, sweat still oozed through my clothes. I grabbed a washcloth and tried to soak up some of it. The cloth was dirty. A black sludge spread across my chest and arms. I didn't notice until I was covered in wet soot. "Is it impossible to stay clean out here?" I asked.

Edgewood smirked. "If I were you I'd keep some fresh towels in my car, to wipe down after clocking out."

He finished stacking steel and then decided to go on break. He parked us on the far side of the new rolling mill, beside a pair of train tracks. An engine clacked by us—covered in psychotic graffiti. We sat there, watching the train and stealing glances at one another. The train's iron wheels ground and squeaked against rails. The cars stretched out of sight, around a bend and into the forest. I tried to count them as they rolled past.

Edgewood drained his canteen and wiped his mouth on a clean part of his sleeve. I hadn't expected to meet anyone like him out here. He looked a little fragile for a steel mill, not as old, not as clay-skinned and lined with labor as the others. With his hard hat off, I noticed the black locks of hair coiled on his head. The texture of his hair reminded me of my mom's.

The longer I critiqued his features, the more familiar he appeared. I recognized the deep lines that arced around his lips when he yawned. The angle of his brow and the shadows they washed into his deep set eyes. I slapped my thigh and laughed. "Hey, I know you. You're the guy on the ceiling tile!"

He flinched. "Whose ceiling?"

"This guy who paints all of these murals around the plant," I told him. "He did your portrait, on a ceiling tile of all mediums. Very clever."

Edgewood gave me a sideways glare. "How do you know it's a guy?"

"Well, you never know for sure. But the work has masculine qualities. Very sharp and clear, straight and kinetic. Lots of tension and violence."

"I see, girls don't do kinetic?"

"My work strives for calmness and stillness. I like unity and stability. After all, I drew about fifty coffee mugs for my senior art project. Gray. No color. Long horizontal surfaces."

"I guess your life must be pretty kinetic, if you find escape in static."

"You could say that."

"Boyfriend?" he said.

"No," I answered. "Girlfriend?"

He shook his head.

I began to fidget with the folds and bunches in my jeans, then I shoved him. "Wouldn't have thought so, given the sexual tension in your work."

His body snapped upright. "What work?"

"Oh, come on."

"You haven't seen anything of mine. You don't even know I paint."

"Yes, I do," I said. "I can tell."

"Yeah?"

"Sure. The way you talk."

Many of the rail cars we saw were smothered with graffiti. Someone had spray-painted a rainbow on one, lightning on another, an eyeball on another. Edgewood commented on each one, explaining that an entire subculture of graffiti artists thrived in certain parts of the state, devoting themselves exclusively to trains. These artists looked down on those who tagged bridges and sides of buildings. For the train artists, moving targets posed a greater challenge. A few had developed reputations. Edgewood could identify their tags, and had seen a few masterpieces steam by over the last year or two. The railroad industry had crusaded against them, however, and one of the subculture leaders had even been bisected by an engine. Another had been shot by an overworked train conductor.

"What do you think about all that," he said, nodding toward the tracks. "Art or vandalism?"

"I guess that depends on who you are." I shrugged. "My dad would say vandalism."

"I know the answer depends on who you are," he said. "I meant what do *you* think?"

"Well, the answer also depends on which rail car," I said. I pointed at one sloppy tangle of spray paint. "That one strikes me as pure vandalism. Whoever did that one only wanted to piss people off. That's not art."

Edgewood frowned and ran a greasy hand through his hair. "Well, I'd say all of that qualifies as art. The kind of art I admire most is always in somebody's face. Art is *supposed* to piss people off. That's the kind of art I like. You don't have to go to a museum. The art comes to you. If you don't like it, tough. That's the whole point of a mural. All these guys who work here, you know? They work twelve hours a day. They go home and sleep, then they wake up and go to work again. What guy's got time to go see art when he works sixty hours a week? Here, the art comes to them. It's philanthropy in a sense."

"I'm not sure," I said. "I've seen one of these murals . . . "

"Which one?"

"Over by the entrance," I said. "The work is strange, I admit, but nobody's really stopping to look."

"Not now, they aren't. Those murals have been around a few weeks. Some new ones are probably going up soon. You'll see whole crowds. I love the murals, myself. They remind me of Orozco, this Mexican muralist. Have you ever heard of him?"

In those days I knew more about art than most people, at least at my high school, but I hadn't heard of Orozco. So I lied. "Sure, of course. I admire his, um, style."

He smiled in a way that called my bluff. "I have a room full of prints at my place," he offered. "Maybe you'd like to come by."

His offer sounded like a date in disguise. I said, "Sounds lovely."

He wrote his phone number on the back of a receipt from his

pocket. "Maybe you can show me some of your work, too."

I smiled without thinking, and quickly directed the smile at something neutral, the windshield wipers. "How do you know I'm any good?"

"You were in the newsletter last week." He smirked. "You won some award at your high school, right?"

"Actually, the award wasn't little," I corrected. "It was statewide."

"Oh, yeah? Congratulations, then. What's next?"

"Art school."

"Where?" he asked.

"I'm going to an average school," I said. Yale had accepted me, not that I should've cared. You go to Yale and brag about it, or you don't and you don't. Even with scholarships, my dad admittedly couldn't quite afford to pay. His salary was big enough to rule out financial aid, but my mom's medical bills had feasted on his bank account. He was still dealing with my mom's credit card leftovers. I had sky-high hopes regarding art school, to impress my teachers and find a small corner in the art world for my work. I didn't want to jinx myself, however, with big talk.

Edgewood smirked. "What's an average school in your opinion?"

"Emory," I said.

"Are you nuts? That's not average."

I shrugged. "Depends."

"Cheer up. You look like somebody just died." His CB radio crackled on the dashboard. Someone's voice stuttered through, telling Edgewood to drive to one of the distant storage yards to load a truck for shipment. "Well," he said to me, "see you tonight." He squeezed the ball of muscle above my knee, but not as hard as I wanted him to. "Going to be okay in this heat?"

"I guess."

He reached down into the floorboard and tossed me a bottled water. I almost said thank you, but decided to save it for something more important.

After climbing out, I stood on the country-fried concrete, watching his forklift rumble off. I tried etching his name into dirt while taking a long dusty walk that looped around the mill and led me to the front gate.

That evening, I spent too long in front of the bathroom mirror and then left for Edgewood's place, so nervous that I almost ran over my dad's mailbox backing down the driveway. I couldn't stop thinking about the mural Edgewood had painted of the skeleton giving birth, wondering how long he'd agonized over details, how he'd given that puzzle of bones such a feminine quality, whether he'd used a ladder or a harness and rope to paint at such heights. I'd never dated anyone whose work mystified me, not even the boy who'd painted my portrait encaustic.

My car crept through the narrow streets as I tried to follow Edgewood's directions. The closer I came to his address, the creepier the neighborhoods looked. Houses leaned to one side, some with cratered roofs, others with a single shadowy figure asleep in a rocking chair. Broken street lamps lined the sidewalks. I could hear the crunch of glass as wire-limbed pedestrians wandered from somewhere to somewhere else. Nothing seemed in any special hurry around here—not the people, not the fog that smudged my vision, making everything hazy and vague. Van Gogh could've signed my windshield and sold it for millions.

I rolled down my window to get a better view of the address numbers painted across the mailboxes, which wobbled in gusts of wind. My directions led me down into a shadier area of town, where the houses were all tall and slim and had tiny front yards, most of them crowded with toys that, by the looks of things, no child had touched in decades.

On the street corner stood a concrete sarcophagus of a building. The structure looked out of place here, mythic in stature, as if a god from some forgotten religion had dropped it here from the sky. I got out and took a closer look at its vine-strangled, crack-veined façade. That's when I saw a plaque, which explained that this place wasn't a house. It was a prison, built two hundred years ago and abandoned a hundred years later. I made a note to come here and sketch this mass of stone, then stood there for a while and enjoyed the quiet. Moths fanned their wings against the glass lamp above the prison's iron door—the only light for blocks.

The iron door squealed open. Then a hand dragged me into the building's liquid darkness.

I stumbled up the steps. I was blind until we neared a single light bulb that dangled from the ceiling, shining like a moon. Vines snaked through cracks in the walls, doorways sealed in black. I must have realized the person who'd pulled me inside was Edgewood, and I never felt any fear. Our feet clicked and popped on bits of plaster.

He led me through a chasm of a hallway. After pushing our way through layers of plastic drapes, we stopped at the entrance of a concrete cave. Still mostly blind, I walked with my back against the wall, moving in inches.

Something snapped.

A padlock?

A circuit breaker.

Edgewood flipped on a studio lamp in each corner. Light sprinkled onto us. The blackness washed into other parts of the prison. When I turned around I saw that my back had been brushing along a decade of the Mexican Civil War. On one wall, faces of Aztec deities hovered over peasant mobs. On another wall I saw baby skeletons curled up inside jars. The colors were vivid. This art played tricks on me, corrupting my ability to gauge distances. The figures defied physics and space. In one mural, a woman's torso stretched out of the sea toward the clouds. She wore eight necklaces and four earrings in each ear, rings in her nose. She seemed like a goddess.

"That's beautiful," I said. "I like the deep contrasts, and the shapes. How did you learn about Orozco?"

"Honestly," he said, "my first memory is standing in front of an Orozco. I was four, I think. My parents had taken me to a museum in Chicago."

Edgewood leaned closer to the goddess sprouting from the ocean and covered her cheek with a hand. I stood by, half jealous, wishing I could become the woman in this mural. Edgewood would fall asleep watching me, and every morning he would repaint my eyes and lips—to keep me from fading.

"I have more on the next floor," he said. "My own work."

We climbed upstairs, where I studied four walls and a ceiling. His art seemed to be a cross between insects and calligraphy. He had simplified Orozco's style, ditching the political symbolism. Orozco's murals incorporated bright hues from the entire color wheel. Edgewood relied on red and black. In one mural, rust-tinted skeletons built a house from their own bones under a violet moon. In another, a sandstone creature reminiscent of a locust climbed through a skull's eye socket.

When he asked which of his I liked best, my eyes stopped on the mural of a girl. She stood in the corner, about a foot tall. The girl was ageless.

She was topless.

She was headless, dipping her big toe into a bloody pond.

"I like this one," I said. "What's it called?"

"Sally," he said. "Do you like it?"

I laid my hand on the mural. "I have no idea how old she is. She could be ten or twenty. No smile, but she's happy. You can see it in her posture, the pert curve in her spine. She's on her tiptoes. But her neck and shoulder turn a certain way, as if she's making sure nobody has followed her here. Her elbows stick out at a certain angle, like she's trying to be quiet. She prefers to be alone."

Edgewood loosened. His hands sank deeper into his pockets. His voice softened. "Thanks."

"I like your art better than Orozco's," I said. "Why do you like red?"

"Red's the color of steel," he said. "In its purest state. I could watch steel melt for hours."

"You make me feel kind of like Sally." I aimed one of Edgewood's studio lamps at her for a better look. She had come to this lake in the middle of autumn, under a canopy of reds, oranges, yellows. Bizarre creatures, cats with goat horns, bipedal buffalos, prowled at the vanishing points of the mural. Another animal that lay tangled through webs of branches above Sally reminded me of Miles Burkholder Carpenter's *Root Monster*—twiggy limbs, three-headed, wide eyes, fanged snarl. Their crimson eyes all twinkled yellow in celebration of death, but they almost smiled at Sally. I perceived that these mystical animals had come here to admire and protect her. This relationship implied Sally herself might not be so innocent.

As I bent forward, toward the pond's surface skin, Edgewood touched my back. He stood behind me, leaning into me and over me, so that we studied from the same vantage point. Our body heat converged.

"You *are* kind of like Sally," Edgewood said, resting a hand on my shoulder. "You should have her." He led me to a utility closet. The door wailed open, revealing rolled up posters with numbers written near the circumference of each. He pulled one out, as if he were unsheathing a sword.

"So, I won't tell anyone," I whispered, as he presented the print to me with both hands.

"Tell them what?" he asked.

"That you're the vandal."

He leaned forward, letting the poster roll into my palms. His knuckles touched my fingertips. "I guess I'd be pretty dumb to invite you over here, if I was worried you would."

"Or you'd have to think me a little slow, not to figure things out." I tried to catch his eyes, but they kept turning in his head. "Does anyone else know that it's you?"

"I don't invite many people over," he said. "The secret stays safe that way."

My fingers plucked at the rubber band wrapped around my gift. "Vandalizing the plant is kind of a dangerous obsession. If my dad found out, he'd fire you. You could wind up in jail."

"I can't worry about that," he said. A beetle scuttled between my feet. Edgewood caught it and ushered the bug through the iron bars of a small window. "I have to do this."

Another beetle crawled up the wall. I tried to ignore it. "Why?"

"Bringing the art to the workers, that's part of my plan. And I feel different when I'm out there in the mill at night, just painting. I feel . . . good."

Wind gusted in, giving me a chill. I rubbed my arms. "How can you stand living here, by the way? No heat, no air conditioning. The idea of living in an abandoned house has a kind of rustic charm, but other than that I'm puzzled. I'm surprised you've got electricity."

"I manage. Plus, I don't have to pay rent."

"Or utilities, I guess. But don't you get worried at night—bandits, killers, the insane?"

"They don't worry me that much, not as much as the ghosts."

"This place is haunted, too?"

The prison had a long history to supply one's imagination with spirits, but Edgewood's favorite story was the tale of Raven Brooster, who between 1798 and 1801 lured a hundred wealthy merchants to her Inn & Tavern on Rainbow Row in Charleston. There she drugged their cider, cut their throats, and used their blood in a sequence of old Gullah spells that would supposedly make her a princess in Hell. According to the story, she hanged herself in this prison shortly before trial. The guards found a relatively brief farewell note tucked in the folds of her dress:

> *Dear Sirs,*
>
> *Please forgive any mess caused by my early departure. Was eager to see if my spell worked.*
>
> *Yours,*
> *Raven*

I told Edgewood that if I were Raven, I would watch out for those merchants she'd poisoned in the afterlife, assuming some of them didn't make it to Heaven.

As Edgewood rummaged through his memory for another story, I thought about kissing him. The fact that he lived in an abandoned prison might be a deal breaker for many people. But despite the exposure to elements and the occasional bug, I could easily pretend I was in a castle up here, married to a duke or a count.

I wondered what kissing him would be like.

Was he a biter?

I slid my fingers toward Edgewood's and leaned forward. Our cheeks touched, followed by our lips.

He placed a hand on my neck. My elbows rested on his shoulders, arms folded across his back.

ON MY WAY HOME, I drove past a meadow of deer, their heads bowed and ears back. They looked Zen, making grass a seven-course meal. To the left of the herd a single doe scrubbed her deep brown flank against an oak, eyes closed and almost smiling. One way to kill an itch, I guessed. My dad always said to honk at crowds of deer to keep them from running toward your car. I did, three times, and their heads sprang up, eyes glittering in my high beams. One deer leapt into the air and scrambled toward the woods, tripping over a log. Typical.

I'd expected to go straight to sleep when I got home, but apparently my night had just begun. One of those wild summer storms blew in without warning. Branches crackled in the wind. The moon sprayed white onto a sprouting thunderhead. When I turned into my dad's driveway, I saw my mom on the front porch. She sat beside a column on the porch floor, legs hanging over the edge, as my headlights made a paintbrush stroke of yellow across her. The wind had turned her black hair into a tornado.

We met outside my car, where she handed me a gift-wrapped book. "Your graduation present," she said.

I held the box at arm's length. My fingernails carved grooves into the wrapping. "Jeez, Mom. You could have used FedEx."

Driving several hours to deliver a package struck me as odd, but that alone might've meant nothing. I knew any slightly unusual behavior could foreshadow an eventual trip to the hospital. And yet false alarms happened frequently. One afternoon a few months ago, for example, I'd come home to find our television lying beside the trash bin. Nervous, I held prolonged conversations to test her sanity. Eventually I asked, "So what's up with the TV?" and she said it was broken beyond repair. After she'd gone to bed, I dragged the TV inside and plugged it in, just in case. Sure enough, nothing happened when I hit the on button. Considering this set was almost as old as me, there were few reasons to consult a repair man.

Now here she was, driving all the way from Marietta to catch up for a few minutes and deliver a gift. Was this a false alarm, or cause for genuine concern? I moved the box under one arm and leaned on the opposite leg.

"How's work so far?" she asked, leaning against my front bumper. "I miss you so much already. I feel like you've been away for months."

"Mom, are you okay? Don't you have to teach tomorrow?"

"Yes." She glanced at her watch. "In fact, I should go. I just wanted to say hello."

We could hear thunder now, distant and rolling. A giant leaf flew into my mom's hair, disappearing in its thick black nest.

"Dad's probably still up," I said. "You want to say hi to him, too?"

"No thanks. I strictly want to avoid your father. He's the one who tapped my phone yesterday, which is why I drove here. They're monitoring calls from coast to coast. So I wanted to let you know in person. If you don't hear from me, the reasons are complicated."

Suddenly, I felt light-headed and dizzy. I backed away from her, tripping over a fallen branch. The wind began to moisten, a sign that rain would soon fall. The sky flickered blue.

In the year since Dad left, I'd learned how to manipulate her out of dangerous situations. I tried now. "Mom, you should stay. Have you slept? It's a long drive back to Marietta."

"You mean am I taking my medicine? Yes. I'm not talking about the CIA monitoring or anything. You must think I'm a nut. I'm talking about the credit companies and such. It was on the news."

She was on a new drug now, but I couldn't remember the name. I'd lived through these spells for a decade and wasn't even sure what her problem was. The doctors had used many terms, changing their diagnoses every month.

"I have to go, Sarah. Do you have questions? Remember. Write, email. Don't call. Oh, and I almost forgot. My replies might be hard to read. They might be backwards and upside down, like da Vinci's code. You should hold them up to a mirror. Don't talk to anyone from the CIA."

"You said they weren't involved."

"Be quiet," she whispered. "I'm trying to trick them. If I keep saying they're not, they'll start to believe it and leave me alone. The power of persuasion."

"Mom, please stay. Get some sleep, just for tonight. You can even cancel class. Students love it when that happens, don't they?"

"I'd like to stay, honest. I just don't know." My mom folded and unfolded her arms and fiddled with a bracelet on her left wrist that kept sliding down, making a tink-tink sound. Something about the watch she wore looked strange. Staring at the analog face, I noticed the hands had stopped ticking.

Finally, she paced back to her car and fell behind the wheel, which she covered with a printout of directions. I knew she wanted to roll down her window and ask for help, either a better map or a place to sleep until her head cleared. I let her go, though, even if that meant her getting lost and winding up in Alabama, like one of the last times she'd stopped taking her pills. I went inside, then spied on her through the blinds as she backed down the driveway, headlights off.

After she'd left, I waited outside my dad's door, wondering if I should wake him. The few times I had, when my mom went off her meds and lurked through the house naked, lighting limbs of furniture with a matchbook or building pagan monuments out of the china, he always looked betrayed. As if I were to blame, as if somehow I'd driven my mom crazy, as if I were now bent on driving him over the edge, too. My hand swirled around the cold doorknob, but I never turned it. Instead, I called the highway patrol. I explained her record. The operator apologized, but nobody could pull over my mom without cause. Trust them, he said. If she sped or drove recklessly, they'd take care of her.

"This woman needs to be strapped to a bed," I pleaded. "If she speeds, she'll just get a ticket."

"Well, if that's the worst that happens, then that's the worst that happens."

I loved the logic of authority.

To calm down, I made hot tea and scouted for a place to hang dear headless Sally—my gift from Edgewood. She looked nice tacked above the mantel, but my dad would've disapproved of covering one of his precious photos of Bethlehem Steel. So I moved her into my room and hung her above my makeshift bed. But she looked uncomfortable there. I wouldn't want to be hung on a wall. Finally I spread Sally on the floor and sat beside her, wishing she had a cheek to kiss. Who knew, maybe to Sally I was a painting, a figure who was still deciding her pose.

3

MANAGEMENT DIDN'T ALLOW CELLPHONES inside the plant. So a little after seven, I hid beside a mountain of rebar in a gravel yard. I'd smuggled mine in to check on my mom. I dialed her number and waited for an answer. None came, except a recording of my mom's voice telling me to leave a message. I ended the call before the beep. She sounded lost on this recording, nervous. I wondered exactly what she'd been thinking about the minute she made that message. I dialed again, then sat on a rusted stack of rebar and watched forklifts roll past one another, drivers waving as they carried rebar from the back of the rolling mill to one of the warehouses. The rebar on their forks wobbled as if any minute the bundles might seesaw and cause the whole forklift to flip over on its side. Watching them from a distance, I was reminded of the circus, the star acrobat who walked a tight rope with a long pole balanced in her hands.

I tried again and again. My mom didn't answer.

I left a message the tenth time, hoping she'd forgotten her conspiracy theories from the previous night. I hoped this was a close call, that a solid block of sleep would clear her mind.

In the meantime, I tried to find something to do. I still had no specific job, so I could go where I pleased. An aimless amble led me to the rolling mill. I stood outside a wide entrance and let the process of steel-making hypnotize me. Only a stone's throw away, hot streams of glowing red metal jetted through at thousands of feet per second, all inside this enormous hangar.

Eventually, I wandered into the shipping end of the plant, where overhead cranes slid back and forth along warehouse roofs, stacking bundles of rebar in wide, tall towers that almost touched the ceiling. A gloved crewman climbed one tower, the steel so hot it made ripples through the air. Once up top, the man waved at the overhead crane operator, who slid toward him and gently lowered three bundles. These warehouses were so gigantic and overflowing with steel, I guessed, that the crane operators needed men on the ground to help them figure out the right place to store a given size and length of bar.

What fun, I thought, what risk, to climb that high. I placed my hands on one stack of fresh steel and groped for a grip, heat roaming my fingertips and palms, and tugged myself up a notch. I leaned into the stack and heat blew through me. Each step and swing of the hand brought me closer to the top, but I could already feel the pads of my fingers starting to blister. My skin was scorched before I'd climbed halfway. A burst of hot wind hijacked my hard hat and blew it out of sight. My hair whipped out and began to tickle my neck.

One of the climbing crewmen saw me from halfway up his own modest two-story crag and shook his head. "Ain't no place for a girl, Miss. Better get your butt down and find your hard hat."

As I searched for my hardhat, the man paused his climb and struck up a conversation. I couldn't imagine what musculature was needed for him to hang by one arm, his hand laid almost gently across the rebar, with his legs straight, boots anchored into the steel. He told me he'd done this for years. His first day he'd had to buy a new pair of work boots: all shift he'd walked sixty foot strips of rebar like planks, guiding crane operators. The heat turned the soles of his shoes into putty.

I noticed his eyes, red-rimmed and bloodshot from long, hot hours. "We got a dangerous job. If you're not careful, you can die from dehydration. If nobody's paying attention you can pass out and lie up here all day, just cooking like an egg." He wiped off a few beads of sweat with his free hand. "I'll tell you what, though. I sure hate that all the textile mills closed down. That work wasn't half bad compared to this."

"Would you like some water?"

He smiled. "Sure, I guess that'd be pretty fine of you to go fetch some."

I passed the rest of the morning by making conversation and offering water to the workers. Stories about the dangers of mill life led my mind away from the question of my mom's safety, and I was grateful.

By lunchtime, my mom hadn't returned my calls so I tried again, but this time my call went straight to voicemail. After leaving her a message, I returned to the outside storage yards and crunched around the mill's gravel plains, admiring the mountain ranges of rebar.

I called again and left another message.

Then I tried to stay busy.

By three o'clock or so, I'd filled up my mom's voice mailbox. I called the Highway Patrol again. They were helpful. They suggested I try calling her landline, her office, the school. I did. Nobody knew where she was. Her art history class had waited fifteen minutes and skedaddled, leaving a polite note on the chalkboard. I tried to call my grandma, thinking she might offer advice, but nobody answered.

I stood outside my dad's office, watching him chair a meeting. Something told me to wait before telling him.

So I walked and worried.

My phone rattled in my pocket.

"Mom?"

"No cellphones at work," the voice said. The voice belonged to my dad.

"How did you know I had mine on?"

"I didn't, until now. I have everyone's personal cellphone number, and a lottery system that selects numbers, a dozen or so a day, all random. I call those numbers. If you answer, we take away part of your incentive for the week."

The incentive was bonus pay based on tons shipped. As temporary help, I wasn't even qualified for bonus pay.

"Mom was supposed to call me this morning," I said. "I'm worried about her."

"Everyone usually is. What has she done now?"

"Oh, nothing," I said. "I'm just being paranoid. Sorry about the phone."

An empty road curved across the distance, calling attention to all of the open space between me and the fence and the no trespassing signs. The other side of the road was all forest. Somebody could've been hiking or even camping out there, picking flowers and making wreathes out of four-leaf clovers. Staring into the green on that otherwise pointless afternoon, I had no idea that three hours later my dad would announce between swigs of iced tea, probably spiked with bourbon, that the highway patrol had pulled my mom's car out of a mess of oaks and kudzu down in the Lowlands. He would shudder as he explained how, as they pried open the driver's side, her body wavered to one side and wilted toward the pavement.

MY DRIVE HOME TOOK LONGER than usual because my focus waxed and waned on the highway. Cars swerved around me, horns jolting my eyes open. Finally back at the house, I fell onto the couch with a bowl of dry cereal, pleased to be alone. I found the remote under a canopy of steel industry magazines, then aimed at the television, as if the control were a gun, halfway pretending the TV was my dad. I fired again and again, amazed at the cable selection. All those channels, and he used three at most.

On one station, a middle-aged man in a kimono brushed Japanese characters onto the back of a nude woman. She posed with her knees folded under her, holding her hair in a bun. The room was empty except for them, white and sterile. The man in the kimono took his time, as if he were engraving her. The woman never moved, not once, not even a twitch. I watched for some time as his paintbrush squiggled along the woman's skin. When he completed two pillars of language, one on each side of the woman's spine, the man inked a price in yen across one shoulder blade. Then the camera panned around to show the woman's dead porcelain face and jade eyes.

She'd been a statue, all along.

Turning, I saw my dad creep into the kitchen from the back door and fix himself a glass of ice tea. "Your mom's dead," he said. "They found her in a swamp."

He back-stepped into the pantry and returned with a bottle of Bourbon, relaying the rest of the news as if he were an anchorman on CNN. He'd left his hard hat on, I noticed.

"What are we going to do?" I said.

"Drink tea. Eat, go to sleep early, and go to work tomorrow. They're sending your mom back to Marietta, where she'll be buried."

Feeling dizzy, I said, "I guess we'd better FedEx some invitations." Then I went upstairs and sat in the shower for a long time, fully dressed, shivering in steam. Eventually I fell down on my pile of quilts, soaking them, and tried to blind myself by staring at the moon too long.

4

THE NIGHT BEFORE my mom's funeral, I opened the graduation gift she'd given me. Sitting Indian style, I snipped tape at the gift's edges and removed the wrapping paper the way a surgeon would remove skin. I had a feeling she'd bought me a book, and my hunch was confirmed. The pages were filled with sketches and photographs of sculptures by Alberto Giacometti. A note from my mom was tucked inside. "Remember the vacation?" I did, one of the few that hadn't ended in disaster. Last December, we'd flown to New York for a week. We spent most of our time in the galleries and museums. Most of them let us stand with sketchpads and charcoal and sketch imitations. At the Museum of Modern Art, we'd passed by Giacometti's famous sculpture, *Woman with her Throat Cut*.

In the middle of the book I found a photograph of the work that refreshed my memory. I remembered now how my mom had stood there last winter, looking at the woman's rebar neck with a wedge sliced out, its beetle body snapped open like a rib cage and lying on the ground, right arm thrown across herself in defense—the hand curiously distorted into either a pedal or a cudgel. We'd flipped open our books and drawn for an hour, forgetting to speak. If sculptures could move, I wondered how long this one would take to actually die, if it would gasp and flail.

Edgewood called twice.

I didn't know what to do about him. My palm cradled my phone. My thumb brushed the numbers that would put us in touch. But I couldn't force myself to press down on them. The idea of a relationship sounded, now, as likely as any hope of speaking to the dead.

I thumbed through the book. Another photograph caught my attention, *The Surrealist Table*: a wide-eyed head on a table, of course, lying beside a hand. A quilt covered part of the head, which looked androgynous. I would have to draw that one some time. For the rest of the night, I skimmed descriptions and criticisms of Giacometti's work and stared into the pictures—sometimes on the lookout for meaning in Giacometti's anorexic pedestrians or in his thunderstorm sketches. I drifted off listening to John Cage and thinking about my mom, who'd always seemed to everyone she knew like a pilgrim roaming through the desert. As I floated deeper into the swamps of sleep I thought I could hear my phone, distant and muffled, as if buried deep in sand.

A FUNERAL IS NOT AN EASY THING to plan, but my dad planned my mom's with horrifying efficiency. In two days he'd pulled a dozen strings, sent out bulk emails and text messages, and managed to spread our sad news to family members across the country. The next morning, before leaving for Marietta to attend the ceremony, my dad and I ate breakfast in silence. I wore all red instead of black. Red had been my mom's favorite color. My dad wore his Brooks Brothers underneath a mechanic's jumpsuit to facilitate, well, I didn't know what. Our gazes had fixed on the stale remains of our pizza from a night or two ago. A fly buzzed in the kitchen window, trapped between the glass and the blinds.

"Can we raise the window?" I finally said.

He rolled a cigarette between his palms. "You're welcome to fool with it if you choose," he said. "If you're getting up, pour me some orange juice. Please."

I poured his orange juice and left him the carton. Sooner or later the fly would escape, so I didn't bother.

"By the way, Dad, what's with the jumpsuit?"

He explained that he needed to meet with a few managers before getting on the road, about a malfunctioning stir coil. I didn't ask him to say it in plain English. Someone's wind chimes tinkled away the minutes. He finished his coffee, and we walked to our cars. Fog cottoned the roads under a sky like rusted tin.

I kept my car in the right lane and seldom drove over fifty-five. I didn't have the desire to speed. So many people blew their horns the first hour that I thought about pulling off to paint a sign on the back of my car explaining my situation. By the state line I'd turned into a demon, seldom going under eighty. On the last leg, I went fifty one minute and ninety the next.

At half past ten I snuck into the church to see a wide empty hall and an ancient pastor who'd fallen asleep across a pew. A Bible lay on his left knee, and a peanut butter sandwich lay beneath his right hand. I couldn't believe the size of him or the church. Stone pillars stretched up to a carved ceiling, which arced out and down into panels of stained glass. The sanctuary was dark, candled. The coffin was closed. I left it so. I didn't know how bad the accident had been or how much of her was left under that cover.

Exploring my purse, I found a wallet-sized picture of my mom on the beach, standing beside a sand sculpture of the Venus de Milo, and I taped it where her head would've been.

I looked at the pastor and decided against waking him. Really, to fall asleep in the middle of a sandwich. And well before lunchtime!

I sat and thumbed a hymn book. A spotlight of white sun beamed down in a far off corner, searched up and down for visitors, and faded. A few hymns later the light came back, to highlight the pastor's sandwich. The peanut butter sparkled, as if it might've been a holy relic. Saint Bartholomew's homemade peanut butter, I thought, and smirked. Anything to keep my mind off the inside of that coffin.

An hour passed, and the man still dozed. Nobody showed. The room seemed to mold itself around invisibilities. I imagined a see-through magnetic man attracting all metals in the room—watches, a silver bracelet on my left wrist (I couldn't remember where it came from), and change from people's pockets as they passed by.

Throughout the two hours I called my dad and other relatives.

Then my phone died from a worn out battery.

Minutes passed. I began to circle the coffin like a starved wolf.

I wanted to open it.

No, I didn't.

Yes, I did.

No, I didn't. Yes, I did.

At noon I wanted to fling open the casket and climb in with her. I had to get out of this place, rites be damned. I rounded up a posse of young men from around the church.

I stopped the first one with a "Hey," then described my situation as my face pinked over. Once our numbers reached three I found a muscular security guard, who tried to console me with jokes about my mom's beauty—something he'd deduced from the wallet-sized picture on the coffin. We carried the casket to its headstone, where two aloof men from the funeral home blinked at us, then lowered my mom down like a bucket into a well. I tried to find out when the gravediggers would come, but nobody knew.

I picked apart a bouquet of roses and dropped their body parts onto the casket.

I treated myself to a picnic in the graveyard, coffee and vending machine fruit salad. I read more about Giacometti and found another sculpture I liked. *The Invisible Object*, a woman strapped into an upright torture machine, her hands cradled around air. Something or someone was meant to be there, in those hands. Or maybe the object *was* there, and we just couldn't see it.

A wrought iron gate stood at the entrance of another cemetery for Confederate dead. Someone had tied a state flag on the gate, and someone else had spray-painted the words "fuck you" over it.

I toured the little concrete pillars that marked bodies. A dead oak spread its branches over them, like a protective mother warning others to stay away.

I strolled.

A doll funeral was in progress near the side of the church when I returned. A boy and a girl leaned over a small coffin, dabbing their eyes with handkerchiefs. They saw me and said, "Don't worry. We're pretending."

The coffin didn't look any bigger than a shoebox. I wanted to ask how they'd made it. The coffin even had a plush, maroon interior.

A plastic woman lay inside, eyes closed. She held flowers at her chest. Her skin had been dusted with gray spray paint. Her lips were a stunning blue, and her eyes were shaded dark purple.

The girl opened a black spiral notebook and read aloud. "We're gathered here today to unite this man and this woman in holy . . . Oh, wait. That's the wrong page." She turned to the back and recited what sounded like a mish mash of Milton's famous elegy and Poe's darkest hours. When she was finished, the boy started to clap. The girl grabbed his hands and told him to show some respect.

She then turned to me. "Do you want to help us dig?"

"I'm not sure that's legal," I said. "Where's your mom? Is she inside?"

"No."

The boy pointed toward the parking lot. I scanned it for movement. I shook my head at him, saying I didn't see anyone. Then I saw that he was pointing a little lower, to a headstone.

"Our dad's inside," the girl said. "He works here. He's a mister."

The boy huffed. "It's minister, Molly. Anybody's dad can be a mister."

I knelt beside the doll in her coffin. She had black hair. I touched her cheek with my index finger. "I'll give you fifty dollars for the doll," I said.

"But we have to bury her," the girl replied.

"I'll give you a hundred dollars," I said. "I mean, this is really special looking. Don't worry. I'll bury her. Just wait here. I need to find an ATM. Okay?"

They said nothing, just stared at me as I got into my car and pulled out. I drove half an hour to find a machine, and I finally found one. I fumbled with my card and took a deep breath, counting the twenties and tucking them into my bag. I ran red lights to get back to the church before the kids left, but I was too late. I searched inside the church. Nothing. Outside, however, I saw a Styrofoam headstone. I debated the idea of digging up the doll. I could easily have made one like it, but that wasn't the point. Whatever I made wouldn't be her.

My cellphone began to vibrate. Edgewood was calling me again.

I wanted to answer and explain what had happened to my family the last few days. Instead, I held the phone with both hands against my chest and waited. A few seconds later I listened to his brief message and wondered what he must've thought about my sudden disappearance from work. My dad didn't have a habit of sharing too much personal information.

My throat ached with unspoken words.

I turned off my phone and smoothed my shirt.

I drove to my mom's house. My dad had paid off the mortgage before the divorce, and he would want to sell the thing. So this might be my last chance to treat it like a museum and not like the object of a real estate transaction. To live in the living room and not assess repairs and depreciation or mortgage rates. The front door drifted to and fro as I skipped the rickety third step to the porch. Nobody had broken in. I knew better.

Just how bad didn't become clear until I'd walked the perimeter of the den. I unplugged a knife from the wall, pulled a hammer from my busted television set. I decided to cover the graffiti as best I could with some old vanilla house paint. My mom had scrawled HONOR THY DAUGHTER up and down the wall, the way a punished school girl would write sentences on a blackboard. I amazed myself, going into disaster mode as I had many times before. Repairing the physical damage let me forget. I could pretend my mom was down at the clinic, would be back in two weeks with meds coursing through her veins. I imagined her walking through the door any minute, singing my favorite song and shaking a new bottle of pills like a maraca.

I threw away things that would spoil. Milk, cream, cheese. Then I threw away things that wouldn't. Soup, soap, ice.

Around five I took in a movie at an old theatre in Marietta where my mom and I'd gone together. On weekends she would sit through the same movie three or four times, from matinee to midnight. Sometimes she paid for each show, coming out between features to have her ticket torn. She liked the sound it made, she'd say. Other times she would forget, or didn't feel like moving after the credits. She loved the way the white names looked as they floated up the screen, so much that she did a series of paintings on the conclusions of movies.

This was funeral day, honor thy mother day. I watched a movie twice but gave up on the third showing. I was a bad daughter.

At eight I drove back to the church with a flashlight but forgot to bring a trowel. No matter. My hands could do it. They caressed the freshly tilled earth, and then my fingers plunged down. Those kids had buried her deep. I hoped not a full six feet.

Not far off, I heard the slush of shovels. I looked up. Good, the gravediggers. Come to bury my mom.

A mound of dirt grew by fistfuls. Meanwhile, the moon rose by two degrees, ten. My fingers hit the coffin's surface. I worked the edge of my hands around to the sides and wedged it out, then flipped it open.

She was there, my death doll. I lifted her out gently and held her to my chest.

A flashlight blinded me. Through the halogen halo I saw a police hat and a holstered radio.

On the spot, I made up a fabulous lie. My little niece had "borrowed" my heirloom Barbie and buried her out here as a joke. I didn't actively collect anymore, of course not. But when a childhood memory winds up in a cemetery, the law should show a little sympathy. The officer snorted, and his flashlight swiveled onto the fake headstone. Then he sighed and told me to make sure I washed my hands before I ate anything. Thank you, I said as he crunched off in the dewy grass. Officers had always been kind. The gravediggers slapped their shovels on my mom's grave and groaned to their feet, making their way inside for a Coke. I held my hands under my flashlight. I looked like I'd just clawed my way up from a crypt.

Over the next few hours, relatives called to apologize for their absence at my mom's funeral. One of my dad's overworked secretaries had made a typo in the directions. Our entire extended family had shown up at Six Flags. By the time they had discovered the problem, many of them had gotten distracted by some of the world's fastest roller coasters. I didn't blame them, nor did I blame the secretary. My dad didn't blame the family, either. But the secretary was eventually fired.

5

AFTER THE FUNERAL, my dad allowed me one day of grieving, none for himself. He went to work. Meanwhile I lay on the sofa, at home. I had still not returned Edgewood's phone calls, and I felt ashamed and guilty for thinking about him between those little surprise attacks made by memories of my mom. I even daydreamed about him. He would show up with white roses and hold me. I almost wished I had brought him along to the funeral, and leaned against him, and rested my head on his shoulder, and wouldn't have been afraid to cry a little. Night came quickly. My dad had apparently decided to stay at work. Sick of inactivity, I pushed myself off the couch and pulled some paintings out of my car, ones my mom had done. I wanted her art to move in with me.

Glad to have some means of decorating the drab walls, I hung twelve of them. Then I sat a hunk of clay on the floor and tried to sculpt a bust of my mom, a simple bust, but I couldn't concentrate. The mass of gray took various shapes in my hands, none of them human. Eventually, I gave up and stared into one of my mom's paintings that I'd hung by the window.

At first glance, the painting looked like murder. Mill workers whipped about in their hot metal bath, as usual. The brushstrokes were quick, vicious. In the background, however, I found quieter images. A mother fed her toddler applesauce, rocked the girl to sleep, and then sat down and sewed quilts by candlelight. Okay, I thought. Her Norman Rockwell side showed through. I could see why she'd started over. That kind of stuff is too popular. And yet she'd left a hint of it in the background. The mother and her daughter looked like ghosts, or maybe they were members of a mill family, keeping dinner on the stove.

The usual itch to clutch a pencil pervaded my knuckles. But the sensation didn't feel natural, more like the addled thirst of an addict. I decided to sketch. My work went nowhere. Normally, when I drew, the sound of graphite on paper soothed and completed. But that night, I could only envision the grinding of bones against bones. After an hour, I gave up. I tried to sleep, but in darkness I could still see my mom's paintings. They peered at me through the moonlight. I got up, thinking I'd close the blinds. But then I remembered my room had no blinds.

I tried covering my window with quilts, but they were tattered. Skull-white light peeked through. I tried covering the paintings, but that only made them look like dead bodies in a morgue. Moonlight could kill anything. I'd loved it for that, until now.

Before the funeral I could've studied the ceiling above my bed and imagined myself ten years in the future, with my own gallery, free to embark on summer excursions to remote hideaways in Europe. My lovers would lie on pillows and watch me paint them, India ink on Mylar in Paris, acrylic on canvas in Venice, oil on linen in London. After the funeral, from the moment I allowed my mom's paintings to devour my wall space, those hopes began to dissolve. Now I could only picture myself in a graveyard, drawing my mom's headstone.

My dad kept bourbon and scotch in the pantry. When I reached for a bottle I found a note that said, "Don't feel guilty." The note was wrapped around the bottle's neck with a rubber band. It might've been for me, or my mom's ghost, or it might've been a note to self.

I'd never guzzled hard liquor before. I'd never had a reason to twist open a bottle of anything.

I swigged.

I swigged again.

I carried the bottle upstairs like a little girl with a stuffed bear, prepared to curl up with it.

Halfway past midnight, I woke to the sound of tapping and imagined myself in a Romantic poem. My mom was going to come back as a raven and squawk at me every night until I was eighty. I followed the sound. I leaned toward the window and saw Edgewood in the side yard, holding a handful of pebbles.

I assumed he wanted to know where I'd been all week, if I hated him for some reason, or feared him. I wasn't sure how to explain. I spied on him through the blanket I'd hung. If I'd had any doubts about him or his intentions, they now died. My heart drummed against my ribs. My neck throbbed with blood.

By nature, I wasn't a nail biter. But my first reflex was to nibble away at my fingers.

Another pebble smacked against my window. Bless his persistence.

I slid open the window and almost sang down to him. "My mom died!" I fell against the sill, realizing how uncoordinated the whiskey had made me. My arms were twizzlers. "Okay?"

I waited for him to stop blinking. Then he said, "Do you want to talk about this later?"

I stared at him. "I don't know."

We exchanged several short, abandoned sentences. Then he began to slowly walk to his car, which he'd parked on the street.

"No," I shouted. "Wait."

He turned, hands in his pockets.

I told him to wait by the front door.

Little did I know how much I'd jeopardized this meeting with my plunge into alcohol. I tripped and fell in the hallway and lay there for some time, terrified at the thought of waking my dad. Then I crawled down the steps in darkness, eyesight aided by a full moon. When my hand reached for the knob on the front door, I pressed my face against the window and almost melted at the sight of Edgewood, who sat on the brick steps.

A deep breath did wonders for my sanity, convincing me that I wasn't so drunk as I was nervous.

I opened the door and let Edgewood in. Immediately he hugged me and said he was sorry to hear about my mom. He felt so nice. I realized then that neither my dad nor anyone else had offered me a hug.

Not that my dad was evil; he just didn't traffic in physical contact.

I made the hug last as long as possible. Each time I thought Edgewood might curtail our embrace, I pulled him closer. Then I began to imagine more than hugging, which made me feel guilty. I let him go. "Thanks," I said, and cleared my throat.

We microwaved some worn-out coffee from five o'clock. "She was a painter," I said, breathing steam.

Edgewood dripped milk into his cup. "Like you."

"Not quite."

He leaned against the island, wincing a little at the taste as he sipped. "How's that?"

"My mom was a factory. I've had some difficulty lately, block. That doesn't normally happen."

We sat.

"Same here," he said. "I had to get out of my house. I've been drawing one thing over and over."

"Picasso used to do that," I said. "When he fell in love with a girl he'd draw her over and over. One ballerina he really got a crush on, you know, and he drew a hundred sketches of her one night. His friends found him in a fetal ball on the floor that morning, surrounded by sketches, moaning." I stopped and pinned his eyes with mine. "So what have you been drawing over and over?"

He reached into his pocket and unfolded wads of paper. "You," he said.

There I was, in portraits. He'd drawn parts of me—a torso, a back, half my face, my legs. I was dismembered across twelve sheets. The ways he'd tangled my body parts made me blush. My mom had drawn me before, but not like this. His sketches made me look at myself differently. My finger lightly traced one. "I'm so . . . sexy. Do I look like that, really?"

He nodded.

We moved to the couch.

I kissed him.

He kissed back.

We undressed.

WHEN I WOKE Edgewood was gone, leaving me alone and wondering how to explain to my dad why I'd slept in the den. My dad eased a tray of pancakes and eggs and oatmeal down on the coffee table, then sat beside me. "Tough to sleep, I know."

"The paintings," I said. "They haunt me."

"Put them in the attic."

"They'll be ruined. Anyway, are you going to work?"

He said yes, and so should I. Out of the question, I thought. I'd need another two weeks to function in daylight. I tried to talk his language. I explained how illogical going to work would be under current conditions. I would be unproductive. I would waste time and money. Might as well recover and return to the workplace in a state in which I could contribute something to the plant and, on a larger scale, the global economy.

Being productive wasn't the point, he countered. Work was the best therapy. Better than him, better than booze. "I know a hangover when I smell one," he said.

He left to shower.

I dug graves in my pancakes with a teaspoon.

On the highway my headlights cast sloppy yellow circles onto a white wall of fog. Near downtown, the fog thinned some, giving me a view of the miniature skyline. A train chugged alongside the road, shielded by dead forest, its trees like frayed nerve endings. A cemetery lay on the outskirts of town, a Confederate flag waving at me over the gray boxes of graves.

My dad met me by the gate with a new chore. My job was to ensure that each of the 30,000 bundles of rebar, flats, angles, and channels had a small plastic tag welded to one end. He explained how cranes and forklifts knocked these tags off by accident, all the time, which made this job about as easy as keeping a thousand leaves taped to trees in November. Bundles of steel also got lost on occasion, meaning that I had to hike through every warehouse for hours until I found them.

He told me to be careful. Sometimes dead spots developed in the electrified railing that powered the cranes. Every so often the cranes slid by, lost power in a dead spot, and dropped their bundles. I didn't want to be under a crane when that happened, he said.

After handing me a clipboard, he ushered me into the land that white-collars had forgotten. All day I dodged cranes and maneuvered by trains that chugged through the heart of the plant, filling the warehouses with smog and their banshee goodbyes. In my first hour, half a dozen workers pulled me out of the way of the overhead cranes.

As the day bled out, I tried to understand the mill's metabolism. In the melt shop I watched lava spill into a red pool. Above, steel dripped down the side of a ten-ton ladle. A titan bulldozer with chained tires rolled in and scooped up a mouthful of liquid metal. I would've filled a bottle with the stuff and brought it home to touch up my mom's paintings, but it would've burned through any container.

"Move," someone shouted.

A crane operator loomed down on me from the ceiling. The crane's magnets drifted above me like an empty swing.

Everywhere I went, somebody was welding. Every time I saw someone welding I had to snap my eyes away. The ice blue sizzles of a torch could wash out the pigments of your irises, my dad had said, singe your eyes white. I never knew why my dad hired so many welders. They crouched around every corner and perched on every rooftop, faces masked. Any one of them could've been Edgewood.

WHILE TYING REPLACEMENT TAGS onto a scatter of old bundles, I noticed a single rail car that sat by itself on the tracks, broad-sided by graffiti. I couldn't read the letters, but that didn't stop me from interpreting the hooks that connected them across the browned iron, speaking to me in tongues. I'd seen three such cars, all victims of a spray-paint vigilante. I asked around and learned that for months my dad had engaged in a half-hearted campaign to stop the painting. The only effort I saw was a sign, stuck into the gravel by the train tracks, that threatened vandals with prosecution.

Frequent restroom breaks relieved me of some of the sun's effects. I found myself staring at random objects for long periods of time. Cranes sliding back and forth across the warehouse rooftops;

a crow that hopped from one hot stack of rebar to the next, squawk-ing his frustration. I could understand. He hopped among the bent pieces of steel that stuck out from the sides of the stack like tree branches. They steamed. Heat washed up from the gravel.

A passerby said my dad was looking for me.

Black powder covered every surface in my dad's office. Streaks marked where someone had wiped a thumb across his desk. Ovals remained where someone else had tapped his fingers. A whole hand-print had been left behind by another visitor, maybe a secretary. My palm fit inside it like the last piece of a puzzle. A typewriter sat on a retired table, webbed in filth. A nameplate lay across the keys, letters blurred by soot. Light shone through his windows only in splotches, giving the place a mottled look.

"You want me to dust, Dad?"

"Maybe later," he said. "I dusted a couple weeks ago."

I nodded at the typewriter. "What about that stuff over there?"

"Some bozo left that yesterday. Anyway, the reason I asked you here is I wanted to see if you were ready to move forward."

"On what?"

"Your training," he said. "Or do you want to keep goofing around and working on your tan?"

I crossed my feet. "Kinda hard to work on your tan in this outfit, don't you think?"

"I was joking."

"Aren't you supposed to smile when you make one of those?"

He checked his reflection in his computer monitor. "I'm not smiling now?"

"Doesn't look like you are."

He cleared his throat. His head moved side to side, cracking his neck. Then he stared forward. "How about now?"

"A little, I guess."

He shrugged. "The mustache must hide it."

"Besides, I'm not sure what my job is at this point. I've been wandering from one chore to the next since I started. Most jobs give you a description of responsibilities or something, like my last boss did. Here are your tables. Go wait on that guy over there. Go fetch some more silverware from the kitchen kind of stuff. You know?"

"Fair enough," he said. He pondered my advice, combing his facial hair with a paperclip. "How about this? Go to the scrap yard. A guy named Edgewood works down there. He'll be wearing a visor, cutting up dumpsters with a blow torch. Tell him I sent you. Ask him to show you how to weld."

THE SCRAP YARD WAS AN EXPANSE of dirt that glittered with flakes of metal.

Edgewood's torch was spitting blue as I explored a path up to him through heaps of tires and rusted sheets of scrap. Without much more than a "Hello, how's it going" he attached a tented visor to my helmet, rolled the torch into my hand, and guided it to the side of a dumpster. We let our flame heat the metal to a golden red and then squeezed the trigger, blasting away the metal jelly.

"Sometimes I enjoy this more than painting," he said. The words vibrated through his visor. "How'd your morning go, by the way? A little hung over?"

"Something like that." I squinted. "Hey, do you mind if I ask a personal question?"

His torch clicked and crackled along with the summer buzz of insects. It sounded like it was snickering at me.

I pressed on. "Did we, well, have sex last night? All signs point to yes, but I don't remember so much, you see, because of the whiskey."

The visor moved up and down—him nodding. Then he cocked

his head to one side. "Whiskey?"

"Oh, I drank quite a lot before you showed up."

"I see."

"Edgewood, are you a virgin?"

"Are you?"

"I asked first."

"And I asked last." He looked worried. Of course, I couldn't quite tell with his mask on. "So?" he said.

I shrugged. "Well, not anymore."

His posture relaxed. "So I was your first? That's good, because you were mine."

"Shut the hell up," I said. "You're serious?"

He shrugged convincingly and bobbed his head, just the right amount of red in his cheeks. In my book, embarrassment is hard to fake. I trusted him.

"So, I feel stupid in a good way. You, well, used a condom and all of that. Right? I was worried you'd turn out to be some kind of seducer. You know, sleeps with a new girl every Saturday? How old are you by the way?"

"What's that got to do with anything?"

I sighed. "Jesus, I can't believe I don't even know how old you are. These are things we should've discussed beforehand. I mean, holy shit, what's your last name even?"

"Crake." He lifted his visor then, smiling a little and showing me his driver's license.

My lips parted in shock. How old? He wasn't even old enough to buy beer.

The torch spat and sputtered in my hand. "Good. My dad really would kill me if you were, say, in your twenties. He'd probably fire you."

He nodded. "We'd be smart to keep this to ourselves."

"My mom wouldn't care. God. My mom. I should be walking around in a black shawl and whipping myself. Yet here I am, justifying sex with you. Anyway, this is probably too much to discuss out here."

"Probably," he said. "Sorry. I didn't think I was taking advantage. I guess I was. We weren't thinking. I wasn't. I might be terrible, doing it with a girl right after a funeral. Do I need to go to church?"

"Do *I*?"

"*Do* you? I mean, normally."

"What, go to church?" I shook my head, then cupped my mouth. "Oh, God. Do *you*?"

"Not really."

"Okay." I sighed. "Really. Sitting there's so boring. I went a few times, but always got in trouble for drawing funny sketches. The priest, the choir. I gave them pointy ears and horns. I was a 'sinner,' they said."

"What happens if you have sex before marriage?" Edgewood asked. "Is that *really* a sin?"

"According to some." I paused. "But if you love the person . . . then it doesn't matter. Which I guess is the issue here." I stopped, eyes on the blue drop of fire at the end of Edgewood's torch—so blue it could've been water. "Do you—"

"I think so," he interrupted.

"Hold on!" I kicked a piece of scrap. It did back flips into the donut hole of a tire. "Let me finish! I was going to say the 'L' word. Wow. Listen to me. I sound like an eight year old."

He whispered. "Sarah, I think I do. The 'L' word and everything. So it's okay."

"I'm not sure. What does that mean? If you love someone, do you have to marry them? I'm not saying that we have to get married. That would sound crazy. I'm just wondering if you can genuinely love someone if you don't plan to marry them."

Edgewood shrugged. "I don't know."

"So what does last night mean?" I said.

"I'm not sure."

"Neither am I. After all, I'm only here for the summer." I looked up at him and grabbed his shoulders. "You know that, right?"

"Yeah, you're going to Emory."

"So I couldn't stay here . . . "

Edgewood lifted his visor. "Nothing's exactly tying me to Columbia."

"But you'd be nuts to move to a new city just for someone you slept with," I countered.

"Maybe. But let's just see how things go."

I nodded. "Yeah. Fair enough, I guess."

Honestly, I was already hoping that Edgewood and I would move together.

I was just too scared to say so.

We stood. I thought about kissing him, but then a forklift or dump truck or golf cart might cruise by and catch us. Or my dad would walk up. I looked side to side, and stepped forward. I kissed him quick and hard, and missed slightly. Our teeth clicked.

I turned away. "It's my fault, you know."

"What is?"

"My mom, the way she died. She drove here because I skipped my graduation and didn't tell her goodbye. I, me. She's sensitive, I'd forgotten. She'd been doing so well on the new meds, and I completely fucking ruined her winning streak. I should've known. A sad book's enough to do her in sometimes, or an argument with my dad."

Edgewood wiped sweat off his forehead. "What do I say?"

"Nothing. Sorry. Wow, look at that huge bulldozer over there, carrying that flaming pile of mush."

"It's called slag," he said. "Runoff from the melt shop."

"We should get to work."

"Yeah, let me show you how to use this torch again." He took my hand and moved it against the rusted metal. A silver line trailed behind our fists.

Edgewood twisted the knob on another torch and fit it into my hand. We worked. My visor's blue plastic gave the day an overcast quality. "What'll happen to all of this when we're done?" I asked.

"They'll feed all of this into the mill, melt it down."

"My dad never talked about this part of the plant."

"The job is a little dull."

I ran a thumb down a fanged edge of scrap. Dead steel, I thought, waiting for rebirth.

Kissing Edgewood at work was a thrill. We hid behind a Ford Explorer's browned husk every five minutes, ducking down at the slightest sound of footsteps or voices.

ALL WEEK WE DRANK COFFEE and traded biographies. That Friday we ate dinner at a nice restaurant followed by fancy coffee and dessert. The café Edgewood picked resembled your typical grandma's house. Two floors, lots of small connected rooms, shelves loaded down with heirloom china. It was the kind of place where you could knit sweaters or confess to murder and adultery and nobody would overhear.

We talked and held hands. I fleshed in some details about my mom's death.

Edgewood didn't excel at this kind of heavyweight conversation. He tried hard, however, and his verbal blunders had an unintended effect on my mood, making me giggle at his misplaced sincerity.

For example, he tried to fill one awkward pause by talking about the death of a pet jellyfish, then a pet iguana, then a pet newt. "I know these all sound trivial," he said, touching my arm with an earnest expression. His eyebrows rose and fell. "I'm trying to work up to bigger things, like my grandma. My great aunt." He took a deep breath and let it out. "I don't know. I give up. Who's more important than your mom?"

"It's okay, Edgewood. We can just sit here. I don't mean to keep blabbing about my screwed up family." Without warning, I choked up a little, but recovered. I guzzled my coffee and tried to casually seal my mouth with one hand.

The thought of bursting into tears before a café full of strangers terrified me.

I reached for his other hand.

We played chess, using crumbs for pieces, which didn't work too well. We reached the bottom of a second cup and went for refills.

That's when I saw my senior thesis on display: a study of pitchers and mugs, hung in the main room. In every drawing, a mug looked to a pitcher for guidance, but the pitcher was always turned away. Obviously, I'm the mug. My mom's the pitcher. Or maybe that's just what I want myself to think.

"Nice. These are yours? I've been looking at them for months. They're like photographs," Edgewood said. He lifted one off its hooks and studied the images. "The lines and edges are so subtle. They almost dissolve into each other. And you have a nice sense of texture."

"Flattery will get you everywhere," I said.

His thumb moved from the lip of the mug to a window in the background. "This one also has a great balance between natural and artificial light."

As he admired my work, I admired him. He looked so nice standing there, almost like a professor, and he possessed a good eye. I wanted him to stop wasting his life at my dad's mill. But I didn't want to spoil this scene. "And?"

"Balancing light shades, that's hard to do in this medium." Edgewood tapped the window sill. "But one little problem. See the clock you drew on the kitchen counter."

"Oh, what about that clock?"

"The hands. They say three o'clock. But that can't be. Look where the sun is in the sky, looking through your window."

He was right. My sun was too close to the horizon, more like five in the afternoon.

His face came closer to the window. "Well, and your shadows don't slant at quite the right angle either. See those little trees?"

"Okay, I get the point. Really."

"You might try ditching the wind. Those drapes look nice in the breeze, but consider your lines."

"Really, thanks. But these drawings are framed. Finished. I can't start picking stuff apart."

"But just listen. If your curtains hung straight down, they'd emphasize the mug and pitcher. More unity that way. See?"

"Christ," I sighed.

"Sorry. Just trying to help."

I couldn't look at these without nitpicking, myself, remembering the little flaws Mr. Anjalu had found in his final critiques. My cross-hatching was inconsistent in spots, and I knew I if spent more than a second admiring them then I'd want to pry open the frames and keep working.

He stroked his chin, regarding me with amusement. "You work mostly in black and white, don't you?"

"So?"

"Don't you find it, well, limiting after a while?"

"No."

He shrugged. "Maybe you should try something new. Do some pastels, or water colors. Yeah?"

"Not my medium. I have so much room to grow before I mess with those."

"What about some screen prints? I mean, you talk about being blocked. Maybe branching out would help. Try sculpture."

"Please," I said. "Hush!"

Edgewood pressed his knuckles against the frame, squeezing my neck with his other hand. "You could reach in there and take a sip of that coffee." He reached into his pocket, pulling out a loose roll of bills. "Are these the drawings you won that award for?"

"Yeah." I motioned for him to put the money away, then I rehung the drawing. For a moment, I watched the various reflections that rolled across the glass in the frame. A lady's reflection walked her husky's reflection across the black and white table. "But, to be honest, I don't know what they're doing here. I thought I gave them to my dad."

"I guess he talked to the owner and arranged a little show."

I sighed. "What a shithead."

"Hey, maybe he meant to tell you. I doubt he was trying to fool you. Come on, he didn't think you'd stop in here for coffee, ever?"

"True, he tends to forget things."

Edgewood poured cream into my black coffee as if a brighter color might cheer me up. "Hey, I wouldn't be so upset. Your work's out there. Your dad did you a favor."

"Except that half of them are gone."

"See, they're selling. You should be proud." He tore open a packet of sweetener. "And you should remind Dad about royalties."

On our way out, he spoke to the cashier. Against my protests, he bought one of the pictures.

"Here's a question." He held the sketch up to me like a mirror in the parking lot. "How come you don't sign your work? There's not a single signature on any of those drawings."

I didn't know why.

THE IDEA OF QUESTIONING MY DAD about my art convinced me to stay at the café for another three hours after Edgewood left. My stomach felt singed by French Roast when I finally climbed into my car. Upon arrival, I found my dad's garage door up. A model train whistle greeted me from inside. My dad waved. He crouched beside a large replica of his old steel mill, welded together from scrap metal.

My work boots landed at his feet. "Dad, I went out for coffee today and saw something strange," I said. "Did you sell any of my work without telling me?"

He was holding two model trees between the fingers of each hand. A box of cabooses and a bag of little plastic mill workers lay on the table. "It's complicated. You see?"

"Why did you do it?"

"I would've told you. I just got busy with other things," he said and planted a tall oak beside the mini melt shop. "You want the money? I meant to send it. We made four hundred."

I shook my head at a miniature forklift. "Those paintings were supposed to be a present. You said you'd hang them up in the living room or in your office."

"Not enough space." He shrugged, and made a circle of weeping willows. "I thought you'd be proud of yourself. Not many people can sell their art. Your work is valuable."

"Dad," I said.

"Yes?"

I dragged my feet through his work area and stood halfway

between the garage and kitchen. Instead of everything else on my mind I said, "You forgot to take off your hard hat."

"Go on inside." He waved me away. "We have other things to talk about."

As it happens, my dad needed help grooming our old home for the market.

"How soon can you get started?" he asked.

"I don't know. Next weekend?"

"How about tonight? You could drive down and head back early Monday morning. I would pay, over time."

"Well, I kind of had plans."

He opened the refrigerator and pulled out a pound of ground beef. "Like a date?"

"Tomorrow, maybe I do."

"Oh, with who?" He sliced open the package and grabbed a handful of the beef, rolling it into a baseball-sized wad of red.

A flake of raw meat fell on the floor. I wiped it up with a napkin. "Dad, I don't have to tell you everything. Do I?"

He twisted on the oven. "Guess not. Why don't you invite your date. In fact, I'll bet you could use a muscular man to help with the furniture. Assuming he's muscular."

He began another hamburger patty, slapping meat between his palms.

I said, "It's Edgewood, Dad. I'm dating him."

His fist closed, squishing the ball into a pulp. "I see. Well, you're right. Edgewood is muscular, like many of us who work at the plant."

"Yeah, I know."

Not bothering to reshape the second patty, he dropped it on the frying pan and snatched a wet rag from the sink. "Well, no need to describe his physique in detail. I suppose you know company policy does allow employees to date, Sarah. But I encourage you to keep your distance from him at work. He's very busy and doesn't need, well, distraction."

"Well," I said. "Guess I'll head out."

"Not staying for dinner?"

"I'm in more of a mood for fish."

Edgewood couldn't meet me in Marietta Friday night. He'd planned to mural the backside of the shipping office. But we were on for Sunday.

AFTER A LONG DRIVE, I parked and dove straight into work on the old house. I painted, cleaned, and reminisced. We'd left our impressions, I discovered. Stains in front of the family television marked where my dad, over the years, had spilled too many brands of liquor to keep count of. A black pothole in the carpet told me where he had dropped a cigarette and left it smoldering when my mom called him from a jail in Memphis, having been arrested for streaking on a tricycle. Another charred strip of carpet reminded me of the time my mom played fire bowling, a game of her own invention. She simply poured a flammable substance over a bowling ball. Then she lit a match and, with a gloved hand, sent the ball rolling down the hallway.

Walls in my dad's bedroom had yellowed from two decades' of airborne nicotine, and they would need stripping before receiving a fresh coat of paint. Or, I thought, maybe my dad could market this place to smokers. Already broken in, he could say. I imagined his lungs, two small rooms like this one that couldn't be stripped and recoated.

What to do with the furniture, I wondered. Aside from my mom's artwork on every wall, I wasn't sentimental about anything. Goodwill and the Salvation Army would collect thousands of dollars in old clothes, toys, board games, and junk. They would pass on five thousand more. Eighteen bags of garbage buried the mailbox by midnight, and I had barely begun.

Saturday came and went. By late afternoon I felt like I'd thrown away the whole weekend, left it dumped by the mailbox in a garbage bag.

I drove to a theatre at sunset, exhausted, and sat through a movie about a woman who kills herself with a voodoo doll. Four stars.

The opening scene shows the heroine, Sally I think, cutting her own hair and sewing locks onto the doll's scalp. The doll seems to be of the Raggedy Ann variety, purple buttons for eyes. As the plot develops, our heroine leads a rather mundane life at a café. Except, during breaks, Sally locks herself in a bathroom stall, where she stabs her voodoo doll with a pair of scissors and shrieks in pain. Eventually concerned co-workers report Sally, who loses her job. Then her boyfriend dumps her. After half an hour of soporific suffering, mostly in her studio apartment, Sally stuffs her voodoo doll down the garbage disposal and drops dead on the dusty tiles. The end.

At a nearby buffet I ate Chinese and drove back to the house. I stood in my mom's closet for an hour, wondering what to do with her clothes. A row of dresses drifted in mud-colored light. I tried on a blouse, watching myself in her dresser mirror, then I took it off. I tried on several more articles of clothing. The fabric felt like snakeskin. I knew nothing here could serve as a hand-me-down. In five minutes I bagged up her entire wardrobe and hauled it to the curb. Next, I pulled a shoebox of black and white photographs from beneath my mom's bed and failed to identify anyone in them except my parents. I threw those away as well, all of them but a picture of a baby in diapers who must've been my mom. Even at that age, she looked slightly pissed off.

Edgewood showed up to help me finish painting the dining room. On each wall, he painted my portrait. Then I came in behind him and painted over myself. Maybe if the new owners of our home look closely enough, they'll see my image, looking at them through a thin skin of vanilla.

6

EARLY ONE SATURDAY MORNING, I sketched my dad's empty hummingbird feeder from the kitchen table. The little birds fanned their wings and plunged their beaks in for nectar, only to jerk back their little heads and buzz off disappointed. Such mornings made me wonder why I'd agreed to spend my summer bowing to my dad's requests in this industrial hellhole. Honestly, I understood very little about him, my family, and even less about my role in this script. Answers to questions like these varied on the day of the week, or something as slight as the angle of sunlight through a window.

When I sketched or painted, I often thought I'd come here to learn something no art teacher (even the great Mr. Anjalu, or my mom) could impart. I knew I needed to study more than coffee mugs and kitchen curtains in order to become an artist. But when I watched my dad's car roll up the driveway, seething and grunting as old cars are wont, I thought I'd come here to prove something to him, convince him that I was worth more than a wad of cash stuffed into my shirt pocket. When I ripped open a paycheck envelope, however, I remembered that I'd come here to save cash for my first year at Emory. I'd also come here, of course, to escape my mom for a few weeks. As things turned out, I had escaped her permanently. At least in one way.

Unsurprisingly, then, the past washed up in my mind quite often, like seaweed and dead crabs.

My mom hadn't always suffered from a shadowy mental health problem. Growing up, she was merely eccentric and rambunctious. Once, for example, I told my mom that my sixth-grade art teacher was introducing us to Jackson Pollack. She aimed a cigarette at me. At first I thought she would shoot it into my eye. I covered my face, and she laughed. "You need to learn Jackson Pollack from someone other than a fat, curly-haired twit. I actually met him once."

"Really?" I said. "What was he like?"

"Fantastic. He tried to screw me right there in the middle of his gallery. When I told him to hang on a second and let me finish my drink first, he opened his fly and tried to pee on me."

My mom was making it up as she came and went, but I didn't care. I encouraged her to embellish this story, planning to tell everyone I knew at school. Then we set off for the hardware store, where we filled a shopping cart with paint cans. My mom paid with her credit card. I loved watching her yank this masterpiece free of her pocket book and present it to the cashier like the miniature painting it was. She'd somehow managed to get one of her portraits on her card, like the Van Gogh Visa I now carry in my purse.

She evacuated furniture from the living room, while I carried the heavy cans of paint. We covered the floor in newspaper.

"This is Pollack," she said and dipped a brush into a bucket of yellow and stood there with it dripping off onto her shoes, which were already splattered with five years of paint. She slapped the air with her brush, and yellow curled off like smoke from one of her cigarettes and stuck to the wall.

"Try it," she said.

I whipped paint across the walls, giggling.

In two hours we turned the room into my dad's worst nightmare.

My mom laughed. "Let's see the look on that bastard's face when he gets home," she said as if reading my mind. Then she offered me my first cigarette.

When my dad arrived he surveyed the damage, then he pinched the cigarette out of her hand and made a tiny caress of her wrist in the process. "This is pretty good," he said. "Reminds me of a room I saw in a magazine last week. You know, Monday, sometimes you have some really good ideas."

My mom smiled, accepting his backhanded compliment the way she accepted the fly or the tiny skull in a still life, and suggested Chinese for dinner.

I remember the takeout dinner as one of the few we all enjoyed. We told stories and fought battles with our chopsticks. I squirted duck sauce into my dad's hair, and he poured soy sauce in mine. We drank espresso in the living room and admired our handiwork from that afternoon. Then I was tucked in.

MY FAMILY COLLAPSED AGES AGO, when I was thirteen. During spring break of eighth grade, we drove to an island near Savannah, off the coast of Georgia. My dad had described the area as one of those paradise resorts they advertise on television, young couples riding horseback on the beach. My dad had rolled my thirteenth birthday and my mom's anniversary present into one vacation super bargain. Only my parents could've screwed up a paradise like this.

My dad didn't want to pay for horses, so we rode bikes. The chain on my mom's Fuji was so rusted that it snapped after a mile. Crouched over a sprinkling of seashells, my dad plucked a surprise paperclip out of his shirt pocket and used it to hook the split chain together. After he'd made a test-run circle on her bike, my mom kissed his cheek and clapped.

Within another mile her chain snapped again. We stopped and waited while my dad crouched over the husk of a horseshoe crab that'd been hollowed out by pelicans a long time ago.

"Damn," my mom said. "What now?"

"We'll use our brains," my dad answered.

She pressed her palm against her side, stretching a little. "We might as well take this one back and get a new bike."

My dad grunted and bent the paperclip over again. After a long sigh he said we should push on without her. No need to spoil a sunny day.

Brushing a hand through her black hair, she told us she would stay put and build a sand castle. Then she plopped down and began bulldozing sand into a mound with her hands, her whole face softening to make her look my age. Sometimes I wonder if she would've stayed happy longer if we'd left her there with her sand. She would've built herself a house from the stuff of the beach, made a paintbrush from dried kelp and fishbone, and turned the sides of seaside restaurants and oceanfront condos into canvases.

When we rolled back through, I expected to find my mom cranky and crisp from sunburn. Instead, I saw a crowd, with cameras and camcorders, gathered around a Venus De Milo. Next to it stood my mom, her arms and thighs a little red but otherwise fine. She stood by her creation, pretending to rest one elbow on the sculpture's head as she tugged down her sunglasses and smiled. Cigarette smoke steamed through her teeth.

BETWEEN SAVANNAH'S NUMEROUS THUNDERSHOWERS, I found a starfish on the beach and carried it back to the hotel, where I laid it on a towel in the bathroom and drew it from every angle. My mom found me under its spell and smiled. "Guess what you can do with those," she said. She called for my dad and asked to borrow his pocket knife. Then she palmed the starfish.

"Don't! You'll kill it!" I flung my sketchbook into the tub, every muscle clenched.

My mom grinned at me as the pocket knife's edge sank into the starfish flesh. It jerked and squirmed as she jiggled an arm loose. It wiggled in her fingers as she suspended it from the shower rod like a tree ornament.

I wanted to punch her in the throat. I wanted to hold a steak knife to her arm, just for a split second, and see what she'd do. "Why did you kill it?" I pouted.

"Don't be silly," she said. "Your starfish is fine, and that arm over there'll grow into a whole new fish."

My arms folded. "Impossible."

"Watch and see."

"How fast?"

"Well. I mean, not this second. By morning maybe." She laughed. "My cousins did this all the time when we went to the beach. Not that we went to the beach that much. By the end of the week we'd tripled the number of starfish on the shore." She wiped the blade and held it out for my dad. "Now, don't you go trying to cut off your arm, Sarah. Humans don't regenerate limbs. Wouldn't it be nice, though? I'd cut my arm off all the time. Yours, too. We'd have a hundred of us running around."

"Joy to the world," my dad said. "You guys ready for dinner?"

We dined at The House of a Thousand Crabs. My dad kept losing track of conversation, nodding at rows of silver tubs filled with the body parts of sea animals.

He flapped a napkin across his lap. "My dad went to a seafood place when he got back from Normandy. He couldn't afford the lobster, so he ordered a cheeseburger and stared at the buffet all night."

My mom scoffed. "I'm sure he could've splurged. If I survived something like Normandy, you can bet your sweet ass I'd break the bank on a lobster for dinner."

"Monday, do you have to swear wherever we go?"

My mom raised her voice a little, tossing her hair at him. "Lighten up. You don't have a gigantic problem with the word 'ass,' do you?"

A table full of old money turned their heads.

My mom tapped her spoon on a glass of water and rose as if to make an announcement. "Excuse me, ladies and gentlemen. But a serious question has come up and I'd like your input. Does the word 'ass' qualify as a cuss word? Do you all mind if I use the word 'ass?'" She pointed at my dad with the spoon when their mouths parted. "Let me give you an example. Last night, this guy fucked me in the ass."

The waiter asked us to leave. My mom giggled and slapped him with a crab leg. "Bring us the lobster," she said. "We can handle it."

One of the old money folks leaned to my dad and asked him if my mom was drunk. He said, "No. At least then I'd understand."

The waiter stumbled through a set of double doors. In a minute the manager hustled over and said to leave the appetizers. Don't worry about the check. Just leave.

"Let's order champagne to go," my mom said. "It's the least we can do!"

Nobody had to usher us out.

My mom clung to the exit sign with one hand, waving like a movie star. "Bye, bye, everyone. We're going home to check on the starfish."

"That would've been a good buffet," he said on the way back to the hotel, pulling into a Wendy's drive-thru.

"You want anything, Monday?"

"No, I'll wait til we get home."

He huffed. "We don't have any food back at the hotel, Monday. You can get it here or get it yourself."

"Fine by me. We can find a hundred places on the boardwalk. And they, sir, serve lobster."

Silence did us in. As the car wheels rolled my mom's smile drained. She started to rub my dad's shoulders, apologizing, but he didn't respond. He took the turns harder, and sped through traffic lights, and almost front-ended a limo turning into our parking lot. The chauffer and my mom exchanged middle fingers. Back in our room, my mom lay on a bed and cried. My dad faked boredom and turned on the TV.

"For the love of God, not NBC," she screamed, and clawed her head. "I hate Jennifer Aniston. Her voice makes me want to pry off my fingernails."

I'd read about the howls of wolves. When people go camping and hear wolves howl, the book said, they often think they're listening to a whole pack. In reality, they're probably hearing a single wolf. Studies on the vocal chords of wolves have revealed highly structured chambers that gave them a rich harmonic sound. The book referred to the sounds as "beautiful" and "haunting." That's why I stayed in the room. And it's probably why my dad stayed. On a good night, my mom could sound like five or six wolves.

When I locked myself in the bathroom, preparing to resume my sketches, I found the starfish all crusty and dried out. I filled a sink with water and plopped it in. To my horror, the starfish dissolved into a murky purple sludge. The arm had gone crisp, too, so I untied it and flushed the severed limb down the commode. My mom might boil me for dinner if she found out, even if this disaster wasn't my fault. So I elevatored down to find a backup fish. Blue orbs of lightning pulsed through clouds on a barely visible horizon, one that separated black from blackest. Light rain surfed on a steady breeze. I found my mom's Venus. It'd waited patiently for the tide, and her now decapitated body was melting into the ocean. I covered my face in a towel, coming to terms with the death of things that had never lived.

Once I reached the sculpture, I found a deformed head on the ground, now a lump of sand. I stood there paralyzed as rain pelted the Venus' breasts until they sagged and then slid off. Slowly I extended my hand and let a finger brush against her sternum. She crumbled. Most monuments do.

OUR TRIP TO SAVANNAH MARKED a watershed. Before, my mom had functioned in society. Afterward, her grip on that stone began to slip. Not long after that family vacation, I came home from school one afternoon to find nothing to eat. By then I should've known better than to bother my mom, but I followed the scraping sound of her paintbrush upstairs anyway. I watched her from the bottom step, making sure she wasn't busy before I crackled in on the rice paper she'd spread across the floor.

She sat in the middle of the room, legs crossed and staring through the window.

"Mom," I said.

Her eyes blinked, and she scowled. "Huh?"

"Sorry, I'll come back later."

"It's too late. What do you want?"

"Just something to drink. We're out of orange juice. Can we get some?"

She flung open the refrigerator door, just as I hit the kitchen linoleum. "Here's some milk," she said, and peered at the expiration date. "Oh, wait. It's gone bad. Oh well." She threw the half-gallon on the floor. "How about some wine," she said and spilled me a glass.

"I'm not supposed to," I said.

"Don't be a nerd. Drink it. Or better yet, here's some beer. One beer goes pretty far. Just watch." She launched one into the living room, just missing the TV.

"And, look, we have eggs. They're yellow on the inside, just like orange juice. Have you ever made yourself an egg shake? I'll show you how." She pitched them at me like grenades and laughed. "Dance, dance!" She threw them at my feet as I did a jig. Then she threw them over my head, making me duck. The eggs exploded on the wall— their yolks, like suns, bleeding sunshine onto the wallpaper flowers.

"Drink those," my mom giggled. "Lick them off the wall, you silly bird." She looked about at the destruction, nodding to herself. "Yes, sir. Looks like we have plenty to drink down here. And on top of that, we have water. I'm guessing you know how to operate the faucet."

When she left, I cleaned. Look on the bright side, I told myself. At least we had paper towels.

By evening she usually had returned to normal, as if a trance had been broken.

During dinner, one night, my dad shoved things around on his plate with a fork and paved a road from the blackened biscuits to the over-salted green beans with his lumpy mashed potatoes. My mom made a less than earnest effort to cook most nights, but we understood. She was an artist, not to be bothered by homemaking. That night, however, my dad seemed especially worked up about some aspect of this dinner. Maybe the biscuits were a little too charred. He sighed and looked at my mom. "So how was class?"

"Fine."

"Did you have to take off your clothes again?"

My mom made a cross on her plate with the silverware. "We've been through this." In those days my mom taught at the community college downtown and posed nude for a studio class. She also posed in private for the new head of the art department, a guy named Ian Plebian.

"Can't they hire someone else?"

"I *want* to do it. Lord knows I've tried posing for you before and to little avail. Sex is one thing, appreciation is another. You fuck me, or you used to. Ian paints me."

"There you go again with the language, Monday, and in front of Sarah." He laid brittle broccoli down across his mashed potatoes, as if a tree had fallen across the road. "Don't see why you've got to get naked in front of everybody."

"Grow up, Martin. Sarah knows we fuck. Don't you, Sarah?"

I nodded. "It's not that loud, though."

He loaded down his plate to take dinner back to his room. "My shows are on," he said, referring to his war documentaries. "I'll see you guys later."

MARITAL HOSTILITY ADDLED my mom's emotions, but some other gasket in her brain drove her to a year of bad judgment. She almost lost her job over seducing a student. Then, when silence became the only language my dad used, she took her credit card, along with my college trust fund, and embarked on an extended tour of all the big museums in Europe. She stayed gone for four weeks and only called once, when an afternoon she'd spent in the Louvre studying a sculpture entitled *The Winged Victory of Samothrace* had made her think of me. The sculpture, of a winged woman as she explained, had been first found in fragments in the 1890s on an island in the Aegean Sea. Her arms, legs, and wings had been pieced together, but no one had ever found the original statue's head. "I just love the Louvre," she said, before hanging up. I should've asked why my mom hadn't taken me with her to Europe, but the answer would've hurt.

After her empty-pocketed return, my mom spied on me from corners and doorways. When she wasn't painting, teaching, or posing nude, she watched my every move. One afternoon, she found me napping on the living room sofa, my arms wrapped around one of her sketchbooks she'd filled with drawings while on vacation. I woke to find her rubbing my feet, apologizing to me in whispers. I believe that moment provided the launch pad for her guilt. This guilt eventually overwhelmed her into a drunken plunge out of a second story window.

I remember that half-hearted attempt at suicide. I'd started tracing every page of *Grey's Anatomy* that night. A flashing red dot in the corner of my eye made me look up. It was like a psychedelic traffic light. Voices sprang out from the side of the house. I peeked through my heavy green curtains and saw paramedics drag a body onto a gurney. I didn't realize it was my mom until she waved and then gave me the bird. Azalea blooms had entwined in her fingers.

I pushed open my window and unhooked the screen, then crept into the bushes.

The paramedics lifted the gurney. They'd folded her arms so her hands rested at her chest. She still held the blooms and looked deathly blue in the strobe of a nearby patrol car.

I shouted, causing one paramedic to jump. Would they let me ride in the ambulance?

No, they said.

My dad drove us down to the emergency room. We watched a doctor grope her body from head to toe, asking if this hurt. Did this? Could she feel this? She lay in a contraption that welded her to a bed. Thinking back, the device reminds me of Giacometti's *The Invisible Object*. The doctor smiled and unstrapped her head. She was free to go. She'd suffered only a sprained wrist and a fractured sense of self-worth.

"I was really hoping to have this amputated," she said to the doctor, and held up her bandaged wrist.

We all glanced at each other.

"Seems coherent for the most part," the doctor whispered. "But she isn't making sense. It's probably nothing, you know. Just shock. But I'd keep an eye out."

I studied my dad. He'd gnawed a cigarette into a peppery stub. The nurses had made a bargain with him: He couldn't smoke, but he could chew.

"No amputation." My mom nodded. "Maybe if it swells."

"Let's go home," my dad said.

She glared at us. "You have no reason to get upset, dear. They do it with lasers, with hardly any bloodshed or carnage. It's outpatient surgery."

In the car, my mom twisted knobs on the dashboard. She played with the heat, the air conditioning. She even tried to turn off the headlights.

We pulled through a McDonald's for a postponed dinner.

My mom reclined her seat in the drive-thru, changing her order five or six times.

My dad's store of cigarettes was depleted. "Maybe we can have your egg salad amputated," he said.

"What are you worried about?" She opened the glove compartment and swished her hands across its contents, flapping through the owner's manuals and pamphlets and tossing them out the window. "Here it is, in big bad red. Amputations covered by health insurance. I guess you'd rather fly to Jamaica and hire a chainsaw."

We spread our meals across the kitchen table, making borders with food. I positioned my extra-large Diet Coke between my mom and me so I wouldn't have to watch her pick the sesame seeds off her bun. I couldn't remember the last time we ate fast food, so I couldn't tell whether she would've done that on an ordinary night. She tried to steal my dad's food several times. I played arbitrator for half an hour, negotiating the release of French fries for cigarettes from a fresh pack.

My dad asked me for a favor before going to sleep. He pulled me down the shadowed hallway and spoke in a low voice. He wanted me to stay with my mom until she fell asleep.

My mom and I sat in front of late night television, lights off. At first I got angry. She spoke in barb-wired sentences. Her words skipped from A to F in logic, circled back to C, and flew across time zones and generations. She confused me with old high school friends. She called me by different names. At random moments she cried. "I miss him so much," she sobbed. "Don't you?" I had no idea who she meant.

I must've fallen asleep before her. The next morning, I convulsed into consciousness and saw her bent over me. "Come into the kitchen," she said.

That's where she showed me her arm. She'd taken off the bandages and gone at it with a potato peeler. The peeler lay in a saucer red with the syrup of her blood. Her skin was bruised and shredded. She hadn't done much serious damage, but I still gasped so hard I thought I'd suck my lungs inside out.

"It's just about done," she whispered. "Only the bone's left. You try. I need all the help I can get. This hand has got to come off, before I catch Graham Greene."

"Gangrene?" I breathed.

She held out a steak knife. I stared at the reflection of her arm in the cutlass steel. I was almost convinced that her arm did have to come off, that she had sawed through everything but the bones.

She closed her eyes and clenched her fist.

"But I need to use the bathroom first," I pleaded.

"No," she said. "I need you now, Sarah." She grabbed my arm and tightened my grip on the knife.

I thought hard for an escape. My finger skated up and down the edge. It was a little dull. An idea occurred. Suddenly the room seemed brighter. "This won't work," I said. "This knife's blunt. I need to go sharpen the blade."

"Where?" she asked.

"A knife sharpening kit's in Dad's closet. I can get it. Don't worry. He won't wake up. I'll be quiet."

Her eyes narrowed. She loosened her hold. "Okay," she said and sat back, folding her arms. "Hurry. The hospital closes soon, and we're out of tourniquets."

My dad was already awake, smoking in bed. I followed the red spec of his cigarette through the dark and told him what had happened. He reprimanded me briefly for not taking better care of her. But we agreed that my mom was now a job for professionals.

"Mom," I said, while my dad dressed. "We've got a better idea. Dad said we'll go back to the hospital and they'll amputate your hand. Okay?"

She wiped a watery eye. "I'll miss painting," she said.

We drove through rain on the way to the clinic, but the weather let up when we parked. My mom kept stopping to watch her reflection in puddles. The only way I could keep her moving was by promising that the doctors there would amputate her hand.

In the waiting room I kept my thoughts on *Grey's Anatomy*. I drew pages and pages. On page ten a nurse escorted my mom down a hall, my dad following. On page twelve I was still alone.

On seventeen my dad pushed open a set of double doors and swayed slightly in the entranceway.

"Where's Mom?"

He knelt beside me, explaining that they were going to keep her overnight.

Our ride home was the quietest ever. I realized I'd hardly ever ridden anywhere without my mom. And home was the darkest and most peaceful it'd been in a long time. So soon, I started to imagine a less stress-splashed life. I drew uninterrupted for the rest of the day. On page thirty I went back and gave some of my portraits a new face.

Mine.

I kept the drawings and called them *Sarah Dissected*, as if that were my new last name.

A WEEK PASSED. In the afternoons my dad picked me up from school and updated me on my mom's condition. "She's very sick," he said. He didn't bother pronouncing the name of the drugs, just said they would bring her back to normal. On a Wednesday, if I remember, we sat in the visiting room, waiting for my mom. I watched an old woman chug milk until a white slime gurgled through her lips. A man played himself in chess, hopping from one seat to the other as he teased one of his selves for leaving a bishop unprotected, or a queen in danger.

After a few minutes my mom ambled out in her white gown and no makeup, and spat a few words at my dad. "Did you bring me some cigarettes?"

My dad tossed her a pack.

Slipping on a pair of sunglasses, she flipped a cancer stick into her mouth.

A thick white bandage covered her wrist. Her movements seemed sleepy slow, and she manipulated her cigarettes with the middles of her fingers or palms, not the tips. Her speech came with pauses between sentences, but the logic had returned.

"I'm not sure what you've gotten me into this time. This place is filled with really disturbed people."

"We know," my dad said. "You're one of them."

She sighed. "One man watches the same bad movie over and over again. Won't let anyone else here have the remote control."

"That sounds familiar."

"He's sleeping right now, thank God." She nodded. "I've made some friends, though. Wilma, I think's her name. She's given me lots of good advice. Her family dragged her here, too. Third or fourth time. She says you just have to smile and play along. Laugh it off." She aimed her dark sunglasses my way. "Who are you?"

I twisted my head around but nobody had come up behind me. Did she mean me?

"I'm Sarah."

She nodded again, with a certain coyness. "Play along is what they say. Okay. You're Sarah."

I turned to face my dad. "How soon will the medicine kick in?" I asked.

No answer.

My mom laughed, for no apparent reason.

Meanwhile, my dad chewed his cigarette and rolled his eyes. "They're not going to let you leave until you start acting normal, Monday. That's Sarah, your daughter." He pointed at me. "You don't recognize her?"

"Nice try. We never had kids."

My dad kept trying. I chose to sample the scenery. The man with two personalities was accusing himself of cheating. Nurses had wiped up the milk drinker and given her a Rubik's Cube so she could tear her mind apart further. A girl my age drew at a card table.

She drew with her right hand, the left lying palm up to expose a deep violet slit on her wrist that I could see from halfway across the room. The girl's hair curtained her face. Paper and charcoal littered the space between those carved wrists. I thought we might have something in common.

After approaching the girl with caution, the way you might a rabid dog, I stole a peek at her sketches. In one sketch, a sculptress twists off her own arms and legs to finish her masterpiece—a clay statue of herself. The statue beamed at her creator, who'd chosen to sacrifice her arm and career for one sculpture. I wanted to say something. I wanted to pull back her hair to see what was on the other side.

On the way to the car, I asked my dad how long my mom would have to stay.

"Who knows?" he said.

"Can we visit her tomorrow?"

He eased his cigarettes out of his back pocket and started to count them. "I guess," he said, "I can drop you off for an hour or two." He tried to smile. "What do you want for dinner? Whatever you want. It's on me."

I didn't want to cause trouble. I named his favorite. Home. Pizza.

"You'll probably need some money tomorrow, in case of an emergency." He unrolled seven twenties.

I must've looked at this money a certain way. He added, "Just hang on to it. Maybe you'll think of something you need or want or whatever."

"Thanks," I said.

I've hung on to those twenties. They wait for spending inside a stale envelope in my copy of *Grey's Anatomy*. Funny how some things you keep accumulate in value. Heirlooms. Antiques. Memories. Every hour I keep the money, however, it becomes less valuable, more useless. I guess that's not my dad's fault. Or the money's.

Not until my dad's car pulled out of the hospital parking lot the next afternoon did I doubt I could convince my mom of anything. I carried a duffle bag of her clothes, a box of coffee singles, a handful of peppermint candy, an envelope of Polaroids from family vacations, and my birth certificate—in case she didn't recognize me again. But as I crossed into the ward, I realized proof had little value where my mom's mind had stationed itself.

I entered anyway, hoping the medication had worked its way into her system, and signed in at the front desk. A nurse led me down a hallway, then she pointed into the recreation room where I spied my mom sitting near a window. She and the mute girl sat at opposite ends of a table, drawing each other. The old man played chess as usual, a mirror propped up so that it cut the board in half. He was competing against his reflection.

I poured myself some coffee and then sat between my mom and the girl, eventually sliding over the birth certificate. My mom ignored it.

I started to sketch. First I tried recreating some scene from my childhood that might jog her memory. Soon I gave up and sketched them.

My mom said, "That's good work, Sarah."

I looked up and discovered that she wasn't talking to me but to the girl. She held the girl's portrait like a mirror. "Think I'll hang this up in my room right now. Do you want a Diet Coke?" On her way to the vending machine my mom let one lazy hand comb its way across the girl's curtains of hair.

I finished my sketch and left it for her, unsigned. I told them to enjoy the coffee.

"Dad," I said to a phone at the front desk. "It's Sarah. Come pick me up."

"Already?"

"Thirty minutes here feels like a day," I said.

My mom remained in the ward for another week, and I declined three chances to visit her. When she returned, my dad threw a welcome-home party. Aunts, uncles, and grandparents from both sides filled our living room and traded funny stories. Growing up, for example, my mom used to sleepwalk into her parents' room and sing France's national anthem. As a teenager, she once snuck a stray cat into the house and painted tiger stripes on one side, zebra stripes on the other. Her last year of high school, she skipped three weeks of school to hitchhike across America, persuading the principal to ignore the absences, and leaving nothing but a note for her parents on the kitchen table. My mom listened to these tales as if everyone were talking about someone else. She nodded along for nearly two hours, occasionally sipping from her nonalcoholic champagne, and before going to bed she washed my hair. Neither of us talked about her condition. No apologies, but maybe some remorse tucked away somewhere.

7

O N A DARK AND CLOUDY MORNING, workers were still tearing apart the old rolling mill. I'd arrived two hours early to sketch them as they lumbered out of dark holes, arms hugged around metallic organs, with black cords dangling like severed arteries. What could've passed for a jet engine emerged from the black sheet of the entranceway, wobbling on the tusks of a forklift. Something crashed, and I looked right. Heat breathed through me as billets began sliding out of the melt shop's mouth, about twenty yards off, slow and red as tongues between lovers.

Everything I drew reminded me of my mom.

My dad came up behind me. "Clocked in already?"

"Good morning to you, too. No, I'm just having fun."

I had no idea how long my dad had been here, or if he'd slept in his office the night before.

Briefly, I pictured him lying down on the floor and sleeping like a powered-off gadget, programmed to boot up at the first sign of sun.

"Want some overtime? I've got a big job if you're up for it."

I slapped my sketchbook shut and said sure. What did he have in mind?

I followed him to a warehouse, where he explained how the new mill had released a few hundred ruined tons of steel, producing mixed-metal angles. Too much carbon in the scrap, he said. Or some-thing along those lines. When he started talking formulas, he drove too far into his own vocabulary for me to follow. All I knew was that something had gone wrong, and he would have to freeze shipment on this product. Worse, many bundles in the same heats had apparently come out fine, which meant we'd have to hunt for the defective ones.

We scruffed through dunes of gravel toward a buzz saw that lay beside a driveway. My dad scooped it up and flipped a switch, making it growl awake. It sounded happy to be at work this early.

"Do like this," he said and scraped the saw against a piece of rebar, showering the floor with red. "You can tell by the shape of the sparks." A constant flow of straight sparks was good. If the sparks scattered, then I should write down the tag number. If the sparks "had a hook" on the end, I should also make a note.

"How do I know if they have a hook?"

"They'll look like sideways Js," he said and handed me the saw.

"I'm not sure I'll be able to tell the difference. You've got to have someone more qualified to do this."

"I do, but he's out of town for a funeral."

Edgewood's forklift rumbled past. My dad flagged him down with his clipboard.

"You busy?" my dad said.

Edgewood scuttled to a stop. His forks descended and clanged on the gritty floor. "Never," he said.

"Good. Help Sarah figure out the difference between straight sparks and problem sparks."

My dad traded seats with Edgewood, then drove the forklift out of sight.

I clanged the buzz saw against a bundle and watched the sparks. They all sprayed in one unanimous direction.

"That one's fine," Edgewood said. "Try the next."

I lowered the saw and clanged it again. Sparks sprang in every direction.

"I was wondering," I told Edgewood, "if you would pose for me."

"When do you want to start?"

"How about this afternoon?"

I wanted to draw him in my bedroom, in plain view of my mom's paintings.

After work, we met at my house. My dad's car wasn't in the driveway, not that it should've been. Edgewood and I took the brick steps at the same pace, as if we weren't just walking inside some house but into our first home. My dad never locked the door, so I turned the knob and pushed. The door squealed open.

Imagine what I saw. Not my dad, only a bleak reminder.

A new piece of art had arrived, a framed photograph in sepia. I didn't see a signature, just a reference to the Library of Congress, War Archives. The piece was called *A Ruined Rolling Mill*, and in it the black speck of a young woman seemed to march, almost, down a set of burned railroad tracks. A destroyed train lay on the tracks, the only thing left being iron wheels. The only things left of the mill were four brick pillars. In the distance, gnarled pines flanked the horizon like an advancing infantry. A little shack cowered in the far left corner of the frame, near the top. A footnote below the image said that this had been the Atlanta Rolling Mill, set ablaze by retreating Confederate Troops. Of course, I thought. Destruction like that had a certain style, could only be self-inflicted.

Edgewood knelt forward and squinted at the woman in the photograph. He covered her with his thumb. "She looks kind of like you," he said, "wandering around on your first day. Remember?"

"She's better dressed than I was."

We toured the den, living room, and study, trying to figure out where my dad would hang this new addition to his collection. Then we climbed the stairs to my room where, just outside my door, Edgewood got shy. "Hey, let me hit the bathroom before we start."

Edgewood took a long time, leaving me to reflect on my mom's paintings. Weeks had passed since I'd brought them home from Marietta, and I still hadn't gotten used to them. They frightened me slightly. They looked hungry. I stared at my sketchpad, its white emptiness growing larger by the second. My hands shook. My back shivered. I doubted I'd be able to draw now. Then Edgewood padded into the room with his clothes in a protective bundle at his hips. He crouched down with his clothes, but couldn't let go. "I haven't done nude modeling before."

"We're okay," I said. I crawled toward him, balled up and twitchy like an injured animal. "You can trust me. Come on." I petted him, his curly black hair.

Slowly, his fingers uncoiled and his clothes sank to a puddle on the carpet.

When he began to roll off his underwear, I noticed one of my mom's paintings. In this one a man on a train track lay bisected, razored down the middle by a wheel. I thought of Hyman Bloom and the split body of *The Anatomist*. The victim in my mom's painting was not quite human. Instead of intestines and muscles, springs and gears and wires spilled out of the caverns of stomach and skull. The image made me think of Edgewood.

I turned to him. "You're wasting your time, aren't you, painting those murals?"

"Are you saying I should give up?"

"I'm just saying they don't appreciate you enough out there. The only reason they even bother to wash it off is because my dad tells them to."

"Mural art was made for the working class. You should read about Orozco."

"Whatever you say, I guess. So, why don't we continue with this portrait?"

"How do you want me to pose?"

"Let's see."

I turned Edgewood into a mannequin, twisting one arm and then the other. I opened his palms, closed them. I leaned his head to one side, then another. I cupped his jaw and turned his head seventeen degrees right, four left. I tried to adjust his eyelids, but that might've been asking too much. Nothing seemed to work. I pulled back and framed him with my hands.

He tried a few more poses and eventually spread himself on the floor. Indian style, I sat beside him, close enough to run a hand down his chest.

The first sketch I crumpled and tossed into the hallway.

For almost an hour, I drew and threw. My hands blackened with charcoal. I failed until five, and then quit. He stretched and dressed and met me in the kitchen, where I kept picturing myself shoving my sketchbook down the garbage disposal.

"Show me what you've done," he said.

"You won't like it." But I showed him anyway.

His face turned the color of bones. He swallowed, sitting there Indian-style with my drawings.

Then I realized what I'd done. He had no eyes, not even sockets. Shadows exaggerated the cheekbones and hips. The knuckles bulged, fingers clawed at his stomach. I'd tried so hard to make him look peaceful and relaxed, that I'd stripped his form of its energy. His limbs possessed no spring, and the angles at his joints were too square, giving his whole body the impression of rigor mortis. Light poured onto his shallow, pallid skin in a white, misty triangle—as if from a halogen lamp in a morgue.

I sputtered. "Say something, Edgewood. Please. Am I that bad? Here, those sketches can't be as frightening as this one." I showed Edgewood the sketches I'd drawn of my mom inside her coffin.

Lower jaw stripped off, eyes wide.

"Interesting," he said, then stood. "But I think you miscounted on the upper teeth." His hands made a dome over his groin. "I have to get ready for tonight."

"Wait, before you go. Will you think about the sketch, and help me figure out what's going on?"

He rubbed his thumb on my cheek. "Nothing's wrong. You're becoming a different person, so you're drawing in a different style."

"I want my old style."

"Your old style's gone. Better get used to this one."

Relatively sure of where he planned to go, I put the sketches away. I handed Edgewood his clothes. When he left, I lay on the carpet and stared at the ceiling, and wished for new hands.

THE NEXT MORNING, a man in charred green coveralls told me to meet my dad on the south side of the plant. I followed him to the back end of the rolling mill, where I saw a new mural. In it a worker drowned in metal, strips of rebar making a turban around his head and torso. The drawing was simple, black lines and squiggles against a bright red background. My dad emerged from a door in the mural's middle. The art seemed to have coughed him up. He walked backwards until his shadow fell over mine.

"There it is," he said, and wiped a finger through his mustache. "The mess is big this time. Isn't it?"

I nodded.

"Folks have been talking about this all morning, say this thing just popped out of nowhere."

"Bizarre," I said.

"See anything strange last night?" When I said no, he shrugged and lit a cigarette. "It's a shame, really. This graffiti's kind of nice to look at."

"You could leave it up. Who would mind?"

"We can't leave stuff like this around work. Think if someone came to our house and painted all over the chimney. Wouldn't matter if the work looked nice or not. Sends the wrong message. If we didn't clean up vandalism that looked nice, we'd have to leave all vandalism up. Imagine what vandals would come here and cover the forklifts in spray paint. We'd be a lightning rod's what I'm trying to say."

"It's not like we have a graffiti writer's chat room," I said. "Do all graffiti writers hang out and trade tips on sweet spots to vandalize?"

"Possibly."

A man in a golf cart rolled up and waved at us. My dad climbed in and waved at me. Then the cart wheeled off.

I stayed behind to stare at Edgewood's mural, hoping he'd recovered from the sight of my mom. A few minutes passed before another golf cart rolled up, driven by a man in a white coverall. He unloaded a pressure washer and plugged it into a hidden socket by the door. As the man screwed a wand extension onto his gun, which looked something like a silencer, I wondered which parts he would erase first, what would come next, what would survive. The man threw a ladder against the side of the building and climbed one-handed; then he aimed and fired. A geyser burst of water shot off the mural's turbaned head. Clean grew like cancer until only a black strip of rebar remained. When he'd finished, moving the wand across the final piece, the gravel under us had turned into a muddy creek.

Turning, I caught a glimpse of Edgewood in his big red forklift hauling ass across the storage yard behind me. Dust plumed from the back tires.

When the man had finished washing off Edgewood's mural, I volunteered to drive the pressure washer back to the maintenance office. He waved goodbye.

I cranked the engine and pursued Edgewood around the plant. We met nose to nose, coming from opposite directions down a path that ran through the repair shop. We were at least a quarter of a mile from the mill's production center. Out here dust and rust settled so quickly the mechanics had practically given up on cleaning. They walked around with stiff rags hanging from their pockets. Three or four mechanics stuck wrenches and oily black hands into the husk of a bulldozer. Another chuckled at something on an office phone. I noticed him through a window made translucent by muck and dirt. The garage doors opened onto a plain of bright orange clay.

Edgewood gripped my shoulder. I played with the golf cart's headlight switch, feeling a little like someone stopped for a traffic violation.

"A little dangerous," he said.

"Following you, or staying up all night to vandalize my dad's mill?"

He said nothing, just slapped some dirt off his jeans and jacket. We left our vehicles parked where they were. They looked as if they were kissing. We followed each other through the museum display of broken-down trucks and manlifts, cracked windshields, and deflated tires. Engines propped on cinder blocks dripped oil onto plastic blue tarps.

"Do you like Jackson Pollack?" I asked.

"So-so."

"Well, no matter. I've got an idea."

We stopped by the business offices, which were housed in mobile trailers on the other side of the billet yard. I checked with a receptionist, who confirmed that my dad had flown to the joist plant across town. He'd be gone for the rest of the day.

A shed by the receiving office contained an arsenal of paint, mostly yellow. It was a special neon, glittery paint called "Safety Yellow," used to coat stairs and railing, parking spaces, potential tripping hazards, and anything that posed a threat. Edgewood and I carried a can a piece to my dad's office, where we unhung photographs and plaques and threw blue tarps across everything. The plaques and certificates made six stacks as tall as our knees.

Edgewood lowered the blinds and tossed me a plastic jumpsuit. We zipped up and discussed our strategy:

"Watch me," I said, and pried open our first can with a screwdriver. I dipped and whipped the air with my brush, my favorite primary color traveling across the room in ropes and lassos. Edgewood took a brush between his fingers and mimicked me. Paint slapped against every surface. It danced and spun. The walls dripped until we decided to show a little mercy.

We slashed fake names on the ceiling and folded the tarps. Then we unzipped and crammed the evidence into a garbage sack.

"Looks like a school bus exploded in here," Edgewood said. "Along with a bunch of bright, happy kids."

"I've got another project for you, something even friendlier." I rolled my shirt up to my arm pits. He stood behind my dad's desk, staring at me like a blank wall. My hand wash-clothed my stomach. "Let me be your mural for a few minutes."

"What if your dad decides to swing by? That fucker's always working. You never know."

"You'll mural the side of a building, but my dad's office spooks you. I'm shocked nobody's caught you, and you're just now getting worried?"

"I've got lookouts who hang around. I get a call when your dad shows up past midnight. That's rare."

"Stop yapping and start painting."

He unbuttoned my pants and shucked me. I was naked from the waist down, pants around my knees.

Edgewood's brush licked my waist black and red, blue and yellow. I couldn't wait to see what he was doing. Paint spread across me. When he finished, he positioned me before a tiny mirror that sat on the middle shelf of my dad's bookcase.

I looked at my new skin. He'd painted my insides—intestines, stomach, liver, and kidneys. I laughed. Edgewood had nailed me. My new exterior would be my rotting interior. I entitled myself *Inside Out Girl*.

The company newsletter arrived later that week. On the back cover was my dad in a plush chair, smiling at the art-massacred walls. A picture of me and my mom from last year had been photo-shopped in. We were standing in the middle of the room with our artist outfits on, arms around one another. A short caption ran beneath the picture: "Wife and Daughter Spruce up Dad's Office." I wondered how long he planned to keep my mom alive through editing.

8

O N THE FOURTH OF JULY, my dad invited Edgewood over for barbecue to "talk shop," as he said. We decorated. I drew American flags on our napkins and sculpted a decent Uncle Sam out of potato salad. I called it, "Tater Sam." Throughout our meal, my dad pretended we were at work. He would not shut up about the plant vandals. Every week, almost, a new mural sprang up somewhere. The plant was losing man hours, since he often had to assign someone to pressure wash them.

My dad cleared his throat and dipped his spoon into Potato Sam's top hat. "Which is why, Edgewood, I'm considering a new position."

"Ooo," I said. "Ahhh. Please, tell us more."

My dad shrugged, pretending not to notice my reflection in a spoon on the table. But I could see it, so obvious. "Plant security manager."

Until now, Edgewood had done little except smile and gesture with his star-spangled silverware that I'd stayed up all night painting.

Edgewood swallowed a gulp of sweet tea. "That's excellent news. I hope you catch these disrespectful hooligans and fire them."

My dad squinted, teeth chomping down on a poor, defenseless ice cube. "Fire? What do you mean fire them?"

Jumping, Edgewood sat down his glass in a spare ashtray by

accident. "I mean, I'm guessing they work around the plant. Maybe they even work for the plant."

My dad strummed his mustache. "Very interesting." He laughed, and I almost choked. Rarely did my dad laugh. "Edgewood, that's very smart thinking." He held his tea up for a toast. "That's why you're the man for the job."

Edgewood and I exchanged worried looks as we all toasted. My dad got up and poured us a shot of bourbon and we toasted again, and again, and again.

"What's my raise?" Edgewood said, slurring his vowels a little.

My dad announced with pride that this new job carried a stunning additional dollar per hour. The really good news, he added, was that this position carried longer hours. Edgewood pretended that he could hardly contain himself. After that eventful dinner, we lined our plates up single file in the dishwasher and then shot fireworks in the back yard. My dad had bought a caseload of fireworks, from Roman candles to bottle rockets, for the sewer-level price of five dollars, from a shop called "Frugalworks: South Carolina's Affordable Dealer!" Most of these bargain brand babies didn't light, and the ones that did fell over and fizzled to death.

"I love that you're promoting Edgewood," I said, striking a match on the concrete. "You'll have the cleanest mill in the world. Do they give you a plaque for that?"

He shook his head, covering one fragile flame with his hand. "Your top priority, Edgewood," my dad said, "is to catch those vandals. I don't care what you have to do, or what you need. My pockets are yours, is what I'm saying."

My hand snuck over to Edgewood's. Suddenly we were holding hands, and my dad could see it. Out there in front of him, my hand looked more nude than a nude's, downright pornographic.

I watched my dad flip open his pocket knife, preparing to operate on a malfunctioning bottle rocket as he knelt in the driveway. "Last week, in fact, some gentlemen from Cartersville came over and took a tour of the plant. We showed them our new rolling mill, and they seemed pretty impressed. Then, guess what happened?"

"They saw the murals?"

"Exactly. They saw that wall of graffiti on their way out, the one by the melt shop. Didn't stop talking about it until we packed them back into their little van and sent them home. I couldn't believe it, all five of them."

Edgewood pitched some firecrackers on the ground. They failed to pop. He stomped on one. Nothing. "Did they like the artwork?"

"They seemed to, Edgewood, but that's beside the point. Isn't it? Shouldn't have been there to begin with."

He smiled, hands in his pockets now. "Guess not."

"Maybe you're just jealous," I told my dad. "The vandal got more attention than you did."

His mustache drooped. He carved a firecracker in half with his pocket knife and studied its insides. "Jealousy's got nothing to do with this."

Minutes later we gave up and watched our neighbors' fireworks, sitting on the hoods of our cars. Green, blue, and yellow flowers bloomed in the night sky. Edgewood shook hands with my dad, who winked and congratulated him on his new job. "Now," he said, patting Edgewood's shoulder. "I imagine you and Sarah want to go off somewhere private." He presented us a bouquet of cash.

"Dad, I wish you'd stop."

He ignored my request, stuffing the money into Edgewood's front pocket. "The only condition is that you must spend it all on my daughter."

"Come on, Edgewood. My dad needs to get some sleep. He's not thinking clearly."

"Actually, I think I'll go watch this documentary I found yesterday. Military fireworks and parades." His eyes reflected an exploding star, just to the left of the moon. "Looked exciting."

As he turned toward the garage door, we navigated a battleground of fallen fireworks to Edgewood's car. "So, where to?" I said and buckled my seatbelt.

Edgewood mentioned a trip to the riverbank. We had to celebrate the Fourth somehow, he said, with or without sparkles.

WE DROVE THROUGH DOWNTOWN, parked near a canoe landing, and knifed our way into the woods. When we reached the water, he suggested skinny dipping. He'd posed for me, now it was my turn to pose for him. We saw a sign that said NO SKINNY DIPPING and laughed. He sat on a boulder, smiling as I dipped a toe into the water. Just when he'd begun to sculpt me with his sandstone hands, a lizard hopped onto my hip and crawled between my shoulder blades. It squirmed and kicked like a toddler as Edgewood plucked it off and dunked it back into the river.

"What, are you jealous of a little lizard?"

"You're too popular," he said.

We'd forgotten to bring our towels, so we air-dried. As we lay, I saw something sparkle through the foliage. Edgewood told me we were looking at the steel mill.

"Who would've thought," I said. "We'll never escape."

"You've been there one month, maybe a month and a half. Try two years and see how you feel."

I started drawing on him with a wet finger. "Why are you still working here? Two years is enough to save up some money and 'discover' yourself or whatever. Isn't it time to move on? You could go to school with me, study art. We could be roommates."

"Maybe you're right."

"Of course I am. I mean, jeez, you live in a prison with a garden hose for a shower."

"Picasso didn't have much better."

"But he wanted much better," I said. "Anyway, you'd have to pay tuition and stuff. Can you afford that?"

"Oh, yeah. I don't pay rent. I've been eating like a refugee. Yeah, I've got a few semesters covered."

"We could work together as models. What do you think? Sarah and Edgewood."

"Exhibit A."

We kissed until we were dry.

Edgewood and I dressed each other and drove back to his prison studio, where we drank too much wine and fell into his bed and lay like burnt fuses. I curled into him and spoke in slurs about my mom's book on Giacometti. "He was a wild fucker," I said. "When he was a kid he had this fantasy, you know. Every night he imagined himself storming a castle. No armies or knights, just him and this beautiful princess and her mother. He would rape them both."

"What? No evil sorcerer? No Sheriff Nottingham?"

"He was the villain. It's nuts, I know. You'd expect a serial killer to have fantasies like that. Not a famous sculptor."

Edgewood's hand crawled between my breasts like a tarantula. "You can see it in his work. Males and females don't get along."

"But in reality he was a total Casanova," I said. "I wonder if he acted out his fantasy with anyone. Some chicks are into that."

"Are you?" Edgewood asked.

"The question is, are you?"

"Do you want me to rape you?"

"That's sweet. You want to know what he did after he raped them?"

"Shoot."

"He'd kill the princess in front of the mother. Or the other way around. He fucked the dead girl in front of her mother. Strangled them both eventually, then he'd fuck them again. For years that's the only way he could fall asleep."

"I used to fantasize about girls with rabbit ears," Edgewood said. "You know, furries."

I moaned.

We talked until one of his candles had made a pool of wax on the nightstand. He was making circles in the revolving door of sleep.

"Do you ever wonder," I said, "what your chances are of going crazy?"

"That's a leading question. Do you? Why would you?"

I shrugged. "It happens. Van Gogh and his ear. Lots of artists and musicians and writers."

"Picasso didn't go nuts and jump out of a window or anything," he said. "Giacometti sounds pretty fucked up, but he was never committed. For every artist that goes nuts or dies in a back alley, another ten live on to a hundred. You know that."

"But don't you worry?"

"Sure. I'm terrified I'm going to rape you in front of your mom and strangle you both."

"Actually, my mom is already dead."

He said we should go to sleep.

Easy for someone who didn't worry about ghosts.

I tried to join Edgewood in unconsciousness but kept thinking about my mom's paintings. They'd started to follow me everywhere.

I drove home.

Firework smoke fogged the roads.

On the way I parked at a nearby graveyard and climbed out, scaring myself into ghost sightings. When I reached a random headstone, I draped a sweater over the name and pretended it was my mom's. Now I could visit her every day without having to drive three hours to Marietta.

9

MY DAD AND I did begin to make progress on the front of family union. Whatever walls he'd built to protect himself over the years slid open to reveal some hidden passageways. Some lazy summer afternoons, especially after the Fourth, he and I shared slightly more than our few usual hours of silence around the house. I remember one such afternoon, in particular, when he'd decided to take his first Sunday off in more than a year, since moving to South Carolina. We talked about the possibility of bowling, but neither of us really wanted to. We batted around ideas and agreed to brainstorm. Eventually, I lost my mind in another book on Picasso, reading on my stomach up in my room. When I looked up, he stood in the doorway and started to talk about Eugene Grace, the famous president of Bethlehem Steel. This counted, as well, as the first time in a while my dad sought me out as a partner in conversation. Here he was, chatting. He'd made a special trip up to my room, just to chew the fat.

"Did you know that Eugene Grace paid his elevator girls four hundred dollars a week? Back in the 1940s that was a few thousand bucks."

"Did you know a friend of Picasso's used to hide razor blades in his paintings?"

"Grace even hired fashion models to come and show his girls how to operate the elevator in a pleasing way. He also made them go to beauty school and learn how to apply makeup."

"If you touched the paintings, you'd bleed," I said. "That was the whole point of putting them in there."

"I wonder if Bethlehem Steel made those razor blades." Then my dad fell silent for a few seconds. He adjusted his belt. His face signaled a sudden shift in tone. Had he really come up here just to chat? "Your mom tried to hide razor blades in the pasta once."

"Yeah, I miss her too." I closed my book.

"Do we ever talk about these . . . episodes?" My dad undid a button on his shirt, then quickly redid the button. "Do you ever feel like you need to talk?"

My stomach spiked with pain, as if I'd been holding one of those razor blades from pasta in my guts for years, and only now was the steel cutting into me. "I'm fine," I said.

"Because, well, I was just thinking about those razors. There's probably a lot that we each know about your mom. It might be good to . . . " His eyes looked about the room, as if these missing words might be somewhere, hiding. "Good to compare notes."

"Here's a note," I said. "Mom chased me through the house with a razor blade once. It makes sense. Picasso's friends cemented razors in their creations, so why shouldn't she cement razors in hers? Put them in the pasta, put them in your daughter."

"Well, you never told me about that," he said, as if I'd cheated him.

"It was for the best."

"Incredible," he kept on. "How old were you?"

"About twelve," I said. It was like a door slamming in my face. I didn't want to talk about this subject anymore. I skimmed a page of my book. "Picasso used to carry a pistol. Did you know that? One time a bunch of villagers were going to beat him up for living with an unmarried woman. He scared them away by shooting at them."

"How did you escape? Did you hide in a closet?"

"Picasso was arrested once, Dad. For harboring stolen property from the art museum in Paris."

"Talk to me, Sarah."

"I am. One of his friends sold him a few African statuettes. Turns out they'd been stolen from the museum."

"Why didn't you call the police?"

I hugged my knees. "Picasso cried when the police interrogated him. In fact he'd stayed up all night walking the town, trying to convince himself to throw the statuettes in the river. But he couldn't."

"Sarah," he said, all of a sudden sounding like a real dad. "I'm sorry things didn't work out the way they should have."

"Picasso was also a fashion designer. He made costumes for ballets."

We retreated to our usual corners.

Later in the evening, Edgewood came over for dinner. My dad and I were both grateful and relieved for the company. We gathered around my dad's steel mill diorama after a microwaved banquet and planted trees the size of fingers. My dad shared ideas on how to tighten security and listened to stories about Edgewood's close encounters with vandals. He scrutinized the details. Edgewood told us another story about his night duty. "I chased one down the tracks, but he hopped on a railcar and I couldn't keep up. Maybe if I'd had a motorcycle."

"Did you get a good look at the kid's face?"

"He wore a mask."

"What kind?"

"The guy wore a bandana, you know, wrapped around his mouth like he was a train robber. So, do you think a motorcycle's in the budget?"

"Wait. A bandana's not exactly a mask. You could make out hair color, forehead. Right?"

"It was too dark. I could say brown, but how many guys have brown hair? It was standard length, like yours."

While they talked I dragged a miniature mill worker through the diorama, feeling about seven years old. I dropped my little figurine into a forklift and shuttled it in circles. It felt like a normal day at work, shrunk to a manageable size. But something was missing. Maybe it was dirt and grime. I made a note to shake some cigarette ash onto everything.

Otherwise, he'd made a lot of progress. Now the diorama boasted a blast furnace, like the old mill in Atlanta. The rocket-shaped building rose twice as high as anything else on the landscape. Four fat pipes shot up the sides, another one diagonal and connected at the top funnel, as if it were propping up the whole structure.

"Do you really need a motorcycle?" I asked. "How about binoculars instead?"

"Sure."

"All right, night vision binoculars. That way you can spot them quick."

I scooted closer to the blast furnace for a better look. Between the four pipes was a spider web of steel beams and ladders. In big mills, the furnace made pig iron that was later refined and shot straight through the rolling mill, no reheat furnace needed.

I looked down at the box his furnace parts had come in. A price beneath the barcode said two hundred dollars. I wondered who else in America would've paid so much to miniaturize his job and keep it in the garage.

I pushed a crane back and forth across a warehouse with my pinky and accidentally knocked over a stack of billets. They toppled over on the figurine. First blood. My dad told me to leave it for now.

Something about the accident, though, struck me. The diorama needed more than soot and death. "You need art," I told my dad. "You need murals."

"I guess," my dad said. He backed his engine into a railcar and hooked them together. "The trains also need graffiti." He hesitated. "Would you like to help me with that?"

"It'll be like our old school projects," I said. "I can start tonight. Edgewood, you stay and help for a little while. Don't run off vandal hunting just yet."

My dad went upstairs to fall asleep watching television. Edgewood and I got right to work. He measured the buildings and cut paper from my sketchbook while I mixed the paints. We talked about which murals to miniaturize and settled on three panels from Orozco's *History of American Civilization*. A shotgun-wielding mob, a cowboy guarding a treasure chest, a riot of lips.

Edgewood drew.

I colored.

I wished everything had been as simple.

10

M Y DAD WAS KEEPING A SECRET from me. I could tell. He took me on a tour of the scrap company, where we watched an assembly line of mallets beat old cars into confetti. Cars rolled in, shards tinkled out and down a ramp. The mallets destroyed a hundred cars a day, he said, pointing to a pyre of Buicks and station wagons. I asked about the car seats and nonmetal parts, what happened to them, and he said they got dumped after high-powered magnets sucked ninety-nine percent of the metal chips out of the heap of car corpse. The remains were sent by boat to China, where peasants sifted through in search of metal slivers, the last percent, for fifty cents an hour.

"Sounds a little harsh," I said. "How do they survive?"

"Same way we do."

"What can they do with that little metal?"

"It adds up." He made a sort of Chinese character in the dirt with his boot. Then he stomped a heel underneath. "The question is," he said, "why don't we do the same thing over here? Take all the homeless people. Give them food, a bed. Pay them a few dollars a day to sift through. That's why the Chinese are going to win."

"If that's winning, they can have it."

"Watch out," my dad said, as a magnetic crane swooped over us and stomped down on a car. Something seemed strange about the car. The model, make, and year, and color. After the rusted husk had fallen into the death trap of mallets, I realized it was my mom's car—or one like it.

A red combustion of sound, like machine gun fire, drowned out our voices.

Next minute I found myself seated on a toilet with my hands over my ears. The only connection between stall and scrap heap was a splatter of grass-less dirt I'd dashed across to get away. The noise had followed me, like the growling in my mom's paintings. No matter which way my eyes turned, they met white. Stalls, floor, the inside of my eyelids. Just white, packed ice. I shivered and buried groans in my throat. I imagined horrible things. I saw my mom's car stabbed by mallets, bleeding and screaming, torn apart. The shreds of the interior pulled out of a crate off the coast of China, trucked to a giant landfill throbbing with identical hard-hatted, gray-uniformed drones. One of them digs a hand into a mound of cushion and tweezers out a porcelain crown with his fingers. He finds another, then real teeth. Others join in. Soon, like paleontologists, they unearth and reconstruct my mom's lower jaw. Somehow they do the math and find out where to send it. My mom's jaw arrives in a brown envelope.

I tear mine off and stick hers on in its place. Like dentures. Smile.

The main plant wasn't far from here. I struck out, assuming my dad had already brushed my absence off and returned to his office.

The road from the scrap company to the mill's main gate seemed to lengthen itself out of spite, but I made it, then found my legs and mind too limp to go on with work. So I kept picking up my feet and trudged down the gravel road.

My slow pace gave me plenty of time to study the mill's dinginess. Makeshift office buildings barricaded off both sides of the strip on which I was walking, tan brick fronts with years of dirt and lime dust and grit ironed into them. I imagined I was traveling through the bombed-out remains of Warsaw.

"Found her," someone said.

A forklift rumbled up behind me. I turned around, expecting to find a Panzer. Instead, Edgewood held a radio to his ear. Static and bleeps sprayed out at us. My dad's helicopter circled overhead and descended, making dust fly in halos.

When the three of us were together, my dad folded his arms. "Didn't mean to scare you," he said. "Just didn't know what happened."

"I got sick."

"Like throwing up and such?"

I nodded.

"What did you eat for breakfast? Dairy products aren't good in the mornings if you work in a mill. Stuff'll spoil in your belly."

"That was it," I said. "Too much milk in my coffee."

"Lactose-free creamer." My dad nodded a little. "Try it sometime."

Edgewood smirked his big dipper smirk. "Or soy milk."

"Or just plain black," I said. The way of a true manic depressive. "Has its bitter charm, you know." I paused. "Dad, what is my mom's car doing out here?"

He frowned and twisted his mustache. Then he grimaced. "That's how things work, Sarah. Steel is steel. That car's no good to anybody now. At least not in its current state. What use is it to get queasy over such things?" He twirled his mustache a few more times, then cleaned his safety glasses. "By the way, come see me tomorrow morning." He squinted. "I have a new position that I think will be useful to you."

I gave him a tired, half-hearted salute. "Ay, captain." And I made my way toward the front gate.

Work ended on a dismal note that day, my thoughts captive to that image of my mom's car. Still traumatized, I bought a chunk of clay at a craft shop and then dropped it on the floor of my bedroom, determined to make a bust of my mom. Because I'd given away my only picture of her, I raided my dad's dresser for photographs and found a suitable one that I laid beside the clay. After three hours, I produced a general likeness, but I gave up before starting on the mouth. I left her speechless in that sense, plus I hadn't done the hair. My fingers and palms started playing at her scalp with leftovers of clay.

If I were serious, perhaps I would've used my own hair to finish the bust of my mom. Instead, my palms found themselves smothering what I'd done. My mom's eyes caved in under my weight. Her cheekbones sank. Her jaw and chin flattened.

The doorbell rang.

I waited, listening to a conversation between someone and my dad.

Then Edgewood appeared in the entrance to my room. "You didn't call," he said.

"What?"

"We were supposed to meet for coffee."

Silently, I raised the bust and tore at the neck. Her shoulders and sternum thudded on the floor, and then I was showing Edgewood the sunken severed head of my mom. I tossed it into a corner and shuddered.

Edgewood back-stepped into a corner and tapped at my lump with the tip of his shoe. Then he stooped and cupped a hand under the chin and folded onto the floor Indian-style. He held the head in his lap and began to knead. We occupied our halves of the room, me facing the window, Edgewood directly under the light. I glanced at him, and I had trouble not thinking of him as a doctor putting her back together, face first. I felt like I was in a waiting room or an OR, hand over my mouth in anticipation, with that clutched feeling you get in your stomach.

He made one last gentle pat with his knuckle at her jaw, then a series of taps with his thumbs along the temples. Then he presented the revived bust. I wanted to ask Edgewood to sculpt a body to go along with it, something to hug.

"It's perfect," I said. "But how'd you know what she looks like? You haven't seen any pictures, not even at the house last month."

"Who?"

"My mom, Edgewood. I was trying to do her."

"I didn't know that," he said. "This is supposed to be you." Edgewood then gripped a hand and pulled me to my knees. "I know something that'll cheer you up. Let's go for a ride."

I would've asked where, but I didn't care.

We drove past the mill, down a road that shot straight forward two miles before turning into dirt and grass. Edgewood said a hundred and fifty years ago the road wound all the way to Charleston, a hidden convoy line for Confederates. People had forgotten about it. Parts of the road had been washed out by Hurricane Hugo, he said. Other parts had been re-conquered by live oaks and swamp weeds. After a mile the road started to look like a tunnel, with walls of oaks on both sides. The deeper we went the bolder the trees got, their branches jabbing into the road's shoulder and arcing over the road. Moss dripped down and tickled the top of the car.

We parked and dismounted, then crunched out onto the gravel. Soon we stopped underneath a bridge, which connected to nothing.

No ramp, no exit. Maybe it'd been part of an Interstate drowned by Hugo, or the beginnings of a project otherwise aborted. I could see that. Build the bridge first, and everything else would come later. Naïve, I thought.

Edgewood showed me something special, a baby raccoon skull he'd scooped up from between my feet. He pressed it into my hand like a gift.

I held on, wondering what to say. "Maybe I can use it for a still life sometime."

"Isn't it cute?"

"In a way, I guess so." My thumb traversed the row of sharp teeth, the oblong shape of the head, and the little crest along the top. I hoped some higher form of life wouldn't find our skulls centuries from now and wonder what we'd been.

"Why did you bring me out here?" I said. "For a bridge and a skull?"

That's when he pointed to the ladder, a modern sculpture he'd welded together from rebar and angles. The thing wobbled under our weight as we climbed the fifty yards to the top and cleared the railing. Steel had a coldness to it, even in a summer night's lukewarm breezes. I guess that's why my dad got along so well with the stuff. Steel was cold and tough and dependable. You could melt steel with tremendous amounts of energy, but it always hardened. Transcending the tree line, I got a full view of the half moon, how it killed the living and brought back the dead. Edgewood's eyes became caves. Then I saw the reason we'd come here. He'd muraled the asphalt surface of the bridge. It was the rest of the raccoon's skeleton, drawn in rainproof chalk. "What are you going to name this one?" I said.

"Not sure."

"Here's a suggestion," I said. "Mural, for No One."

"You don't like it?"

I hugged him, and felt like sobbing. "It's beautiful," I said, "but who will see this?"

Edgewood shrugged.

I whispered. "The answer is in the title."

"A point in time came for me," he said, "when I realized something about myself. You remember that prize you won? I won something similar. I did pretty well in school. But my last year I lost my appetite and then couldn't sleep."

"Okay."

"Not surprising for an artsy little shithead. Right? But then I had this blowout fight with my dad. He kicked me out, more or less. One morning, soon after, I sat down to draw. But I couldn't stop thinking about who I'd show this drawing to and what this person or that would say. A week went by, two. Nothing. I couldn't draw. I mean I did move a pencil across a page. I did murals. But people stopped being impressed by my work. So I just had to quit cold turkey for a month. School, everything. I couldn't stand being around people anymore."

"I see."

We sat, holding hands as he continued his story. Eventually, Edgewood concluded, he gave up on high school altogether. He missed most of spring. He still didn't draw.

"Then, I applied for a job at the mill. And this kind of miracle happened. I loved the work. I loved talking to the people. Just a few weeks in, I almost couldn't work for painting. I was happy, you see? I can paint when I'm here. The mill, I don't know, inspires me."

I squeezed Edgewood's hand, pushed his hair back. "Me, too, all of that. But come August, I'm going to Emory. I can't paint *Mural for No One*. It would kill my mom, what's left of her, you know?"

"But do you paint just because your mom wanted you to?"

I climbed into his lap. We rocked. "I don't know," I said. "Guess that's what I have to figure out."

That night I was visited by a new nightmare. In the nightmare, I'm the daughter in the castle. Giacometti comes for us—straight from Hell, no longer human but a disfigured stick figure, an anorexic sleepwalker, like one of his late works, with a swordfish nose. After strangling my mom he climbs down the staircase. He spares me. When he's gone I find a piece of chalk and outline her before she disappears, leaving nothing but the white silhouette that is slowly eroded by rain.

THE HORIZON VOMITED UP a pink blob of sun. Another beautiful day. My dad and I sat in his office, beneath his wall of plaques. As he explained, I was scheduled to work B Shift for several nights, four in the afternoon until midnight. The change started today, so I could go home and do whatever I wanted until then. This job was referred to as "side kit man," though temporarily I supposed we would call it "side kit *girl*."

My dad arranged three cigarettes in a U on his desk. "A side kit looks like this from the rear end of a truck. We make them out of plywood and steel slats." Flatbed trucks are used to ship the steel out to construction companies. The plant saves money if those flatbeds stop by scrap dumps on their way back. Side kits were like collapsible fences. "It's been a major safety issue with us."

He leaned back, fingers of both hands touching at the tips, as if he were making a roof. "Sarah, do you know how your mom really died?"

I rapped my fingers on his desk. "Traffic accident, like you said. Hey, when are you going to start telling people she died?"

He lit one cigarette on the table by touching a match to it. He let it sit there, curling smoke up from his desk before he lifted it to his lips. Gestures must've meant no comment.

"In detail, I mean," he said.

"Please, give me a break. I don't want details. Can you imagine that maybe I wouldn't want details?"

"Only technical details," he said, keeping me seated with hand held up in defense or justification. That meant stop in some languages. "She died in a traffic accident involving a scrap truck. A sheet of iron crashed through her windshield. She was partially at fault, speeding and reckless driving."

I could picture it, my mom swinging between lanes and cursing the driver. In her state of mind maybe she'd thought my dad was driving that truck. Or me. In reality the truck hadn't belonged to either of us. The driver's feet had danced between his brakes and accelerator to keep from plowing through her little Buick as she cycloned about on the highway.

My dad bent over a printout and read through a pair of bifocals he rarely wore. "It didn't help that pieces in the side kit were damaged." Some of the wood had cracked under continuous acceleration and braking.

"I'm not the best person for this job," I said. "Trust me. I'm not a morning person, but I'm not a mourning person either. I'd like to move on. I don't want to be one of those people who gets involved in brain cancer fundraising after a sister passes away or something."

"This'll help you grieve," he said.

"I didn't have to know all of that," I interrupted. "You chose to tell me, and what difference does the information really make? Maybe you feel guilty somehow, that technically speaking she died in a steel mill related accident. But what isn't a steel accident? Cars in general are made out of steel. And airplanes. Plane crashes could qualify as steel mill accidents."

"True," he said. "But you need to get past. I can tell you're still grieving. It's been over a month."

How long is someone supposed to grieve for a parent, or an estranged wife?

"And you, Dad. What are *you* doing to move on?"

"Work."

My job filled up an entire five page, saddle-stapled booklet. Page one showed a flatbed truck. Welcome to Cayce Steel. This manual will tell you everything you need to know about the side kits, their usefulness and weaknesses, and what materials we use. It was informative. I read through twice and then considered my shift composed of discrete tasks. Trucks would drop off their trailers at my side kit station. I would inspect each of eighteen plywood boards. Anything splintered or warped would go into a dumpster. I would also throw away any bent steel slats. I would replace damaged parts with new.

Ensconced in my golf cart that night, I played with my new CB radio, listening to the foreman who told jokes and stories and sometimes sang. Half the time I had nothing to do but drive or stroll. Most often I parked on the far side of the mill, where I heard only the backgrounded drum-splash of steel working itself to life. Even then, I sometimes had to plug my ears to quiet a freight train's long harmonica goodbye.

That night, my dad found me in the plant's repair shop, which looked that night like someone had played Frisbee with old tires. Welding machines, wood boards, rags, engine parts, pipes, and wires were strewn on the ground.

"Watch out for snakes," he told me, "especially copperheads. We do our best to keep them under control. But a few weeks ago a fellow got bit out here."

"Good thing he had his boots on, I guess."

"If I were you I'd start to carry my cellphone and a backhoe."

"I thought cellphones were banned."

"Changed my mind."

"Yeah, why's that?"

He scratched at the numerous award patches on his jacket. "My decision about cell phones aims at family values. I want our workers to be able to communicate with their families in case of emergencies." He coughed. "I hadn't considered that in the last policy." He retrieved a pair of nail clippers from one pocket and cut a loose thread off his sleeve.

"Sounds like a good plan," I said.

He walked down through the dirt, which was sprinkled with chips of metal.

Later that night I jumped back at what first looked like a snake. But it didn't writhe or hiss; it rolled. A twisted slither of rebar. I sat down with it in my hands, tracing its loops. The rebar made me think about Giacometti and *Woman with her Throat Cut*. I drew two lizards concluding an act of vicious sex, the female chewing off the neck of her handsome partner. I decided to entitle this, *Postcoital Munchies*.

11

SOME MEMORIES I FIND still lying around in the present tense, like broken glass on a bedroom floor. I'm fifteen. The entire year boils down to me drawing in my bedroom on late summer nights with the door locked. My mom's been slinking through the blacked-out house all day. While drawing I imagine what's going on in other rooms. My dad sprinkles cigarette ash into a toilet bowl, most likely, where he sits when nervous. He's called the police four times, but they won't come pick her up unless she hits one of us.

What's worse is she's figured out how to unlock our doors with q-tips.

No. What's worse is that I have to creep down the hallway so I can use the bathroom. Slow and careful so she doesn't see me.

Or, I should say, so that I don't see her—naked with strange patterns painted onto her face with mascara.

A slow walk down the hall, through the black air. My mom could be anywhere or everywhere. I can hear her breathing, but can't judge the distance between us.

As I step into the bathroom, I turn and see her crouched, fortunately far off in the kitchen, like a dangerous animal whose attention you don't want.

I close the door gently, preparing to spend the night there if I must.

I'm so scared I don't turn the light on. Instead I feel my way through the cold black, hand along the counter and then swimming out toward the bowl and then easing onto it. I even try to pee slowly so it doesn't make as much noise.

I remember a dozen failed attempts at vacations, and they all blur together, if I'm not careful. And I dislike being careful anyway. So when I think of these trips, I tend to combine the best parts into one or two stories. The Savannah trip, and a visit to some place like Panama City. After an hour of howling on her bed, my mom wouldn't go to sleep. Every half hour she microwaved a bowl of water and touched my sleeping dad on the shoulder. "Do you want this soup? If not I'll see if it'll fit on the most wanted list."

"Go to sleep, Monday."

We could do little or nothing for my mom from a hotel room. We'd made sure she brought her pills. But at the end of our first day, when asked, she'd claimed to have left them by the pool. My dad had spent a full two hours peering into potted ferns and palm trees. He even tried digging at a few places on the beach, figuring she'd hid them in a sand sculpture as one of her jokes. My dad's mood dropped like an Alaskan thermometer. From his perspective he could've spent those two hours relaxing in a hot tub, thinking about how wonderful steel was.

So my mom wouldn't sleep. At close to one in the morning she woke me up and offered "soup." My dad lay snoring with ear plugs.

"I'm going for a walk," she said. "Stay here and make sure he doesn't leave. I don't want to chain strangers to bedposts."

"Wait, I'm coming with you."

Our walk lasted the rest of the night. I followed her along the beach. I didn't mind it, with the ocean's monotone applause and cool wet wind. On her knees, my mom tried to stuff some seaweed in her mouth, but I stopped her. "No," I said, as if to a toddler. "This isn't food." Holding her hand, I pulled my mom onto her feet.

"But I'm hungry," she said, and I believed her. She had refused meals since breakfast.

She tried to eat shells, too, and a crab. I couldn't stop her before she'd scooped it up. The crab pinched her index finger, and she dropped the thing, tearing up. She sat on the sand, holding her injury and sobbing like a five-year-old. I rubbed salt water into the blister to fight infection.

"Who are you?" she said, as if I'd just fluttered over from a flower petal. "Are you a fairy?"

"No, I'm Sarah."

"Good name for a fairy."

I led her to a sidewalk and then to an all-night diner, where I realized she had no shoes and therefore couldn't go inside. I told her to wait while I ordered food and brought it out. Of course, she didn't. As soon as I placed the order I turned to see that she'd left. I followed her voice, to a parked motorcycle chained to a stop sign about a block down. She was trying to find where to insert the quarters to start the ride. A splatter of middle-aged men laughed at her, making vulgar compliments. I handed my mom her chicken sandwich, and we returned to our hotel.

Even classy getaways like Savannah or Panama City hide a little Myrtle Beach tourist trap feel near their hearts, and that's where we'd wound up, on a strip of tattoo bars and 24-hour diners. Empty tourist shops glowed with neon signs. Their windows were patchwork quilts of beach towels. A few drunken bikers whistled at my mom and me, asking if we wanted a ride. They wore nothing but giant bandanas around their waists, like diapers, and the cops on the street corner seemed okay with that. We walked on, my mom's hand in mine. I kept my eyes on a Waffle House up the road. Someone was being thrown out by two night-worn patrol cops.

Someone chucked half of a surfboard through a night club's side door. It skidded to a stop at a dumpster, causing an alley cat to bristle and scurry. My mom wanted to stop and retrieve the board but I kept us on task. "Eat your sandwich and keep walking," I said. "It's too late to surf."

"Where are we going?" she asked, scraping mayonnaise off her bun with a pickle.

"To the hotel, Mom. We have to get back before Dad starts to worry."

"Don't call me that."

"I didn't call you anything."

"Yes, you did. You called me Mom. Why can't we go home? I'm tired of the beach, and a hurricane's coming. I can see it. And look at how sunburned I am. I'm absolutely falling apart. I'll never hold up in a storm like this."

She caked mayonnaise on her forearm.

"Mom," I said. "Don't. That's not sun lotion."

"I'd like to make sure our car hasn't been struck by lightning. Jesus, look at how sunburned I am."

I swear. She wasn't sunburned.

"Our hotel's that way," she said, pointing in the opposite direction. "Unfortunately, they're sold out. Maybe next year."

That's when I gave up on words. I felt like my dad. I just wanted to inject her with something so she'd go to sleep and stop scrambling things up. Understanding my mom's speech under these spells of madness was like watching a three-year-old try to build a house out of chopped-up Lego blocks. Her sentences simply didn't fit together.

Food must've calmed her mind. Back in our room, I convinced

her to lie down. I sat beside her and tried telling a bedtime story. I held her hand a little while, and she didn't mind. I'd never watched anyone fall asleep before, and the scene was pleasant to sketch. With her eyes closed I could pretend she was normal. I remember falling asleep on the balcony, watching the ocean slide up and down.

No family vacation could end without a day devoted to the souvenir shops. Even with my mom's mind unraveling before us, my dad insisted. "Anything you want," he said, peeling twenties from a fat roll. "Within reason. No pet squids."

I loved window-shopping. Shark's tooth necklaces, shark's tooth rings, shark's tooth dentures, shark's tooth bracelets, shark's tooth anything. Beach hunk calendars, plastic models of killer whales, stuffed lobsters and seagulls piled up in barrels. Custom license plates, as many pairs of sunglasses as people on the beach at any given second. You could find anything you didn't need in a place like this, at triple the normal price.

My mom cooed at shelves of blown-glass animals. In particular she'd fallen in love with a mother dolphin and its baby. They leaped in one smooth arc in and out of imaginary waves. She cradled the sculpture against her chest, then hid it in her purse and smiled at me, a finger over her lips. I wouldn't have said anything, but then she hid another pair of dolphins in her purse. When she slipped the third crystal sea animal into her skin-tight Hawaiian shirt pocket, I scouted for my dad, who was having a smoke on the patio. The souvenir shop had a manta ray on display in a fish tank. It hovered, black wings flapping, and seemed curious and excited about my dad's cigarette. It was following him as he paced up and down the deck.

"Mom's shoplifting," I whispered.

"Well, tell her not to. We're about to head out."

Before I could carry out the wise orders an intercom voice asked for my dad's presence at the counter, where my mom waited with a purse bulging with stolen animals.

My mom gripped my dad's collar. "I want them. Please."

He hefted the bag off her shoulder and rummaged through. The animals clinked together like ice inside a cold drink.

The cashier's grimace practically burst as my dad made a thick layer of twenties on the counter. I hadn't seen either of my parents ever so content.

He held her hand to the car, and for the rest of the ride home my mom tossed her new crystal sculptures out of the window. Each time she shouted "You're free!" I listened hard for the sound of shattering glass on the highway. The sound would've been beautiful, but it was paved over by car horns. The last one she tossed was the mother-daughter dolphins, which cracked the windshield of a Durango behind us. A patrol car flagged us down five miles later. My dad treated the ticket like a sunken cost, part of the vacation. My mom never made it home. Halfway, my dad made a mysterious call from a gas station. On the outskirts of Marietta we pulled right into the parking lot of the familiar cinderblock building. At the last possible second, as the nurses escorted my mom through the familiar double doors, I slapped a sketch into her hands. Dolphins had never looked so weird. The one missing a fin was her.

My freshman year of high school was a big lie. Every weekend I invented excuses to avoid sleepovers and parties. At lunch I did more listening than anyone else in the whole school. When semi-friends asked questions I answered with single words and shrugs. Nobody learned about my real family. I spent a good deal of time questioning my own sanity. If I accidentally carried the wrong notebook to class, I thought I must be going crazy. Only a mad woman would take a green folder to physics when I'd clearly marked my blue one. Any time I didn't know the answer to a question, I was inches away from a breakdown. I was ranked fourth in our class of five hundred. Fear does a brain good.

My mom's sanity was always in question. If she forgot some item at the store, like spaghetti sauce or crackers, we both submitted her to torture sessions of questions. Sometimes I wonder if we didn't drive her into her episodes. I remember one Saturday we ganged up on her, interrogating her amidst unemptied grocery sacks. Their plastic handles stuck up like rabbit ears.

"Mom, whole milk was clearly written on the grocery list. We never get skim. Why would you even consider that a possibility?"

"Shit happens," she said. "People make mistakes."

My dad shook his head. "Skim always has a different color cap. You simply couldn't mistake one for the other."

I agreed, opening a sack to see what else she'd screwed up—like maybe the wrong brand of TV dinners. "I hardly think a normal person would mix up skim and whole."

"Have you been taking your pills?"

"Yes."

"Show us."

"How the hell can I show you?"

"Take one now."

"I just took one this morning. You can't take more than one in the morning and one at night."

"How do we know you took one this morning?"

She slammed the cabinets and threw a bottle of them at my dad. "Fucking count them if you want! There's thirty-six in a bottle."

I sighed and held up a plastic bag of sweet potatoes. "Mom, what were you thinking? These weren't even on the list."

She squeezed her head, pacing off. "I can't stand this!"

Anything she did that year became a target. If she drove somewhere without advance notice, my dad went out looking for her. Even
when sane, my mom grew agitated and unpleasant. She snapped and
bickered. What few friends she had came up with excuses to skip
dinners and small gatherings. We were all cruel and unforgiving.
We had daily conversations about her condition while she folded
clothes or tried to paint. When she wandered into earshot our voices
sank, and our eyes darted about. Our shoulders scrunched together,
and we leaned closer. I guess you could say that my dad and I almost
bonded that year.

Any stranger who walked in on one of our conspiracy sessions
would've tagged me and my dad for the crazy ones. We scrutinized
every offbeat word or misinterpreted reference that escaped her
lips. Maybe this wasn't even paranoia on our part. In a way we were
getting revenge.

At least one night a week my mom snuck into my room and
shined a flashlight in my face, trying to turn the tables. "What have
you two been talking about?" she demanded.

"Nothing," I said. "Just take your pills and go to sleep."

"Christ," she said, the beam of light shaking in my face. "Fuck
you, Sarah. One of these days I'm going to kill myself. I can't stand
living like this."

"Don't be so paranoid," I lied. "We're not talking about you. Now
leave me alone. I have school tomorrow."

The more we talked about my mom, the more suspicious she got.
The more she spied, the more we talked.

My dad and I crossed further into her territory. Every day we
invaded her upstairs room, where she painted, and we analyzed
her work for signs of illness. My dad, in particular, encouraged her
to stop painting mill deaths. "Why can't you do flowers and forests,

or beaches? That kind of work sells. People aren't interested in this sick stuff."

Granted, my dad never thought much about my more disturbing sketches and oils. After all, teenagers have an excuse to be a little screwed up in the head.

He asked her to stop wearing so much black. Only the depressed, he said, buy black clothes all the time. He brought home floral dresses and solid blues. When my mom crammed them down the garbage disposal, we threatened to haul her over to the familiar cinderblock building.

"Just leave me alone," she yelled, breaking dishes. The sink filled with jagged wedges of china. "I ought to divorce you both."

During my freshmen year in high school I also decided to stop telling my mom much about anything. I trace it back to an afternoon near Halloween. I was on the phone with a boy. My mom had stepped outside to pet a squirrel. Even in her bad times, they still frolicked for her because she soaked her fingertips in syrup. Three fuzzytails nibbled at her hand as the boy, I forget his name, asked me embarrassing questions, like was I a virgin?

Fifth, I said.

Did I want to come over for his pumpkin carving party?

Sure.

Did I want him to carve my pumpkin?

Give me a break, I said.

I leaned against the door, closing it. The squirrels startled at the sound and bounced off. The door exploded open, sending me halfway across the living room. I fell over the back of the couch. My mom steamed in the doorway, haunting and terrifying and beautiful. "Don't you dare lock me out of my house, you little bitch."

My muscles folded shut. I hung up the phone and didn't call back.

That night she blew into my room again, this time with a candle that made her skin bright orange. She could've passed for a jack-o-lantern.

"We didn't talk about you," I said, covering my head with a pillow.

She sank onto the edge of my bed and stroked my leg through the quilts. "You've gotten so pretty," she said. "I'm proud." She leaned over me and placed her candle on top of my alarm clock. Now we were both jack-o-lanterns. "So do you have a boyfriend these days, Sarah? We never talk anymore."

I told her about one or two dates, nothing big. I decided to bury that day's events.

"You can tell me, Sarah. Have you been having sex?"

"No."

"I see. Are you a lesbian?"

"Mom . . . "

My dad's shadow flowed into the dim light of the doorway. "Monday, it's a school night. Leave her alone. Go to sleep."

For some reason she killed the conversation as requested, without a fight, and blew out the candle.

I don't remember that Thanksgiving at all, except for the priceless image of our baked turkey soaring through the kitchen window. We had no wishbone to tug-of-war over that year.

Arguments and fights doubled in frequency during the holidays. Then one bright spring morning all of our hard work paid off. My mom confronted me as I was leaving for school. She barred my way through the front door and said, "What did you do with Sarah?"

I said nothing. Hell, I was almost happy. For five or six months till then we'd lived under a guillotine. We'd treaded water. We'd waited at the apex of a roller coaster. Choose your metaphor. Now we had a way forward. Something was happening, and maybe in less than twenty-four hours we wouldn't have to sleep with our doors locked and a phone under our pillows. I'd wanted a bagel for breakfast but didn't want to push my luck. I whipped around and fled through the back door.

After school I came home with plans to inspect my mom, but the house had tucked her away somewhere. What I didn't understand quite yet was that something different was happening in my mom's brain this time, a new clash of chemicals. Something blacker, less harmless, less human. Back meshed with the front door, I scanned for signs of her, but all I saw was furniture and empty space grayed by closed drapes. A little sun beamed through and roamed about like searchlights.

Something worse than fear held me in place.

Movement in the corner.

My mom had somehow snuck up from behind. She seemed to emerge from the wall, stepping into this world from another.

A stringy, wet object dangled from her hand. She held it between us like a dirty sock though it was anything but.

It reminded me of a spinal cord.

My words splashed up my throat. "What is that?"

"I can't tell you," she said. "You'd inform your superior."

I called my dad and waited for his car to wheel up the driveway.

Climbing out, he grimaced at me, then headed for the outside steps that led up to our house.

"Don't go in there," I said. "I don't know what's going on with her this time, but it's not good."

"Your mom seems to think you're from outer space."

After two hours we gave up trying to talk sense into her. We spent the rest of the evening hiding in our rooms.

My dad tried to convince the police to do something. But according to state regulations, only my mom could make the decision to stay in a ward, unless she broke the law somehow. My dad's cigarette smoke hit the receiver so hard it bounced off. "She's just built a tent in the living room," he said, "and she thinks my daughter's body has been stolen by aliens."

"That's not against the law," he was told.

My dad hung up after five minutes of useless conversations and walked out of our safety zone, down the hallway toward my mom's tent in the den. He was hoping to cause trouble, I could tell, by the snarl under his mustache.

"Take your pills," he said, and rolled them through the flap of the tent's opening. "Or we'll have to drag you to the sick hotel."

I stayed in the hallway, gawking until my mom's eyes caught mine. She sat with her legs under her, drinking a Diet Coke.

"You need to go home," she told me. "Or I'm going to call the police."

"Go ahead," my dad said. "We'd love you to do that."

She screwed the cap back on her Diet Coke. "I know what you want to do. Shoot me in the head, that's what, and then both of you would be happy." Her eyes teared up, and she shielded her face with her hands. "You'd be so happy. Wouldn't you? Please, I don't want to take the pills." She kicked the bottle of mood suppressants across the room. They cart-wheeled to a stop at my feet.

Police came out of pity. When they arrived, my dad asked me to go upstairs. I watched from the top of the stairs as two officers smoked my dad's cigarettes on the front porch and listened to his story. Then they dropped their butts on the concrete and followed him inside, their handcuffs tinkling like shop bells. Their voices rattled fine china in the cabinets when they spoke. They asked my mom how she was feeling. She answered in single syllables. I couldn't even see her, but I could see the officers as they closed in on the doorway to the living room with their blue Cadillac bodies. I crouched out of sight, behind the stair railing. Behind bars.

I saw a female officer who'd kept quiet the whole time, her fingers locked behind her back as if she'd been handcuffed. The officer slouched against a wall, hips out. Then she pulled her gun from her holster and started to spin the chamber, probably out of boredom.

One of the Cadillacs parked himself on his knees, pulling up a flap of the tent. He nodded, lips in a frown of appraisal. He either liked the color camouflage or thought my mom was hot. "Miss, is your daughter upstairs?"

"No," my mom said. "She's dead. The thing hiding up there only looks like her." She explained what I was but couldn't explain why aliens would do such a thing. "What did we ever do to them?"

The officer adjusted his frown and looked up at my dad. "We can't arrest somebody for sighting UFOs and stuff," he said. His radio crackled. The sound made my eyes jump awake. My mom flinched. Then the officer looked at his partner, who rubbed his chin. "Replaced by aliens. Isn't that like some kind of horror movie? Maybe she's just sick, been watching too much TV or something."

My dad's hands jangled change in his pockets. "Our situation's a little more serious than that," he said. "Trust me."

The woman said, "I don't mean to be rude. But would you happen to have anything caffeinated around here?"

My dad called up to me. "Sarah," he said, "start us a pot of coffee."

"My mom doesn't watch horror movies," I mumbled on my way to the kitchen.

The partner raised his hands, as if my dad had just produced a gun. He suddenly became a hostage. "It happens. You know, after I play Grand Theft Auto on the weekends I wake up Sunday night and swear to God somebody's stolen my car. But no, it's just some kid speeding by."

Coffee percolated. Our three guests continued discussing

horror and science fiction, trying to trace the source of my mom's hallucinations.

The coffeemaker growled out steam, its glass globe full of bile. I poured everyone a cup. The slouching officer accepted hers with both hands and stared into it. She looked exhausted, eyes unfocused and highlighted by black, saggy crescents beneath. I asked if she was all right, and we began to talk. The woman bloomed, as if nobody else cared that her infant had cried all night, so loud and long she'd begun to feel hate. She snorted. "Honestly, I thought about throwing him in jail, just to shut him up. How bad's that?"

"I feel that way about my mom."

"Bet you do," she said. "You know, life is sure some box of truffles, ain't it? Just like in that movie, except my box is empty."

"You deserve better," I said.

Gradually, our attention retreated from my mom's madness. The officer talked at greater length, telling me about domestic disputes and knife fights she'd broken up earlier that evening. She narrated her long, panicked days as a single working mother. Strange that she was an officer and yet still feared the idea of nights home alone. The impression I developed was that criminals didn't terrorize her. Something more sinister lurked about her windows—loneliness, depression. That she'd wasted her life, and maybe even her second chance. That her children would grow up and leave her all alone in her small house, only her faded uniform and a gun for company.

"And to think that I could've joined the FBI," she told me, then looked up with wide eyes. "For real. You don't believe me?"

I dumped a packet of cream into her cup at her request. "Why didn't you?"

"I married some asshole instead. Now I got one kid in preschool, another that hangs around my stupid neck. My hubby's gone. Lucky him. I'll never get out of here."

An officer helped himself to our cabinet and poured my mom a cup. He approached her tent as if it were a cave with a grizzly inside. "Are you going to stay in that tent, miss? Is this protection from the aliens?"

My mom hissed. "Stay back," she said, "or else."

"Holy crap," he said. His cup tipped back. The scalding brown brew gushed over his knuckles. "Or else what, miss?"

"You drank the serum, you moron. Now you're one of them. She snatched your body. I tried to warn you. Now if you take one more step, I'm going to take your gun and shoot that alien in there. Then I'm going to wage war."

He tried to shuffle back, but she crawled forward on her hands and knees, one hand slithering out from the tent for his gun. Her hand moved out like a cobra's head, fingers curled like fangs, and snapped for the trigger. Before she knew it, though, a cuff slapped together on her wrist. I covered my ears, which proved pointless. My mom pleaded in single words—nos and don'ts—as the other cuff chinked together. The scene was stunning to watch, my mom pressed onto her stomach and the female officer's knee against the small of her back.

"Police brutality," my mom hollered into the carpet. "Where's Sarah! I want my daughter! What did you do with her? This is a conspiracy. I swear to God. Please don't let them turn me into a Martian. Someone help me. Help!" She kicked and twisted as they hauled her out by the arms.

My dad crawled into the tent and started to unhook its support frame. The camouflage tarp crumpled. When the support was gone the tent's skin draped over his head. He looked like a paramilitary ghost. I uncovered him. "Let's go to sleep," he said. I knew he meant me, not him. He would try to rest, but he'd wind up on the toilet for most of the night, flicking ashes into the bowl.

VISITING HOURS WERE A CHORE. Somehow my mom had streaked her hair purple. Nurses said she'd stolen bleach and Kool-Aid from the clinic cafeteria. She wore eye shadow thicker than usual and had smeared toothpaste across her cheeks and forehead, giving her whole face a glittery sheen. She didn't have to tell me. I found her playing chess with Mr. Multiple Personality Disorder from last time. He had an advantage. Four knights, four bishops, four castles. Two queens. Two kings. His pieces filled half the board. My mom said it was the only way he would share the game.

"I'm glad you came," she whispered as Mr. MPD made his second move that turn. "We need to discuss phase three."

"Of the invasion?"

"Shhh." She touched a finger to her lips. "Not so loud. These people are nuts, but they can still hear. And they spook easy."

My mom skipped her bishop forward two spaces, mistaking it for a castle. Mr. MPD jumped it with a knight, check mating her at the same time.

"Good match," she said. "For an earthling. Come with me, Sarah Pod Three. Let's go for a walk in the garden. They have several bizarre species of plants and humans there. It's beautiful."

We stepped outside. Everything was dead. Crisp black rose buds drooped from bushes, and years of dried leaves matted the edges of the brick walkway. The trees were small and looked like scarecrow skeletons with scoliosis. Their trunks curved in an S. My mom walked over to a corner and petted one.

We walked in an oval, halfway through which we encountered another familiar face. The suicide girl, same crimson slits except they'd healed up some. The black-red had gone pink with scar tissue.

My mom admired her from afar. "See what I mean? Fascinating. This one's my favorite. I've studied her for days. She doesn't speak.

I'm wondering if she has some kind of defect. Then again, her hand-eye coordination is impressive. She draws well. Look."

The suicide girl looked like a part of the damp stone bench that held her scrawny frame. Birds could have crapped on her hair and shoulders, and I'd have bet she wouldn't have even asked for a rag. A single sheet of paper lay between the girl's hands, which I lifted. It was another Venus de Milo. The girl had drawn arms and legs, hands, and fingers, but that was it. She'd drawn the missing parts, scattered on the ground. In my head I gave it a title. *The Answers Come in Pieces.* This made sense. After all, we were dealing with the Greeks.

We continued on our oval.

"Mom," I started. "I've got a question for you. If the plan is to impersonate humans, why the makeup? Shouldn't you look normal?"

"I do my best." She stretched her shirt up to her chin and scrubbed. The toothpaste faded. Of course, she couldn't do anything about the hair. I actually liked it. She'd done a nice job. She looked like a vocalist for a Goth band. "How's that, more human?"

"Better. Bend down a little." I picked some renegade gunk off her eyebrows. "What's phase three?"

"Getting me out of here, that's what." She reached into her back pocket for a list of supplies that would help her construct a death ray that could cut through the hospital walls. It was actually a grocery list from a few weeks ago. Milk, eggs, ham, a six-pack of soda.

"Can you do it?"

I folded the list into my jacket. "Sure," I lied. "I'll drop everything off later tonight."

"I love you so much, Sarah Pod Three."

12

MY MOM REGAINED CONTROL of her mind for a few months and stopped claiming that I was an alien. Our routine returned to normal. I finished my second year of high school, and once classes ended I prepared to ride off to Georgia's Summer Program for the Arts—a big achievement. My mom threw me a going-away party. She invited my friends, and managed not to embarrass anyone.

I thought our life had climbed a rung or two up from the gutter.

But the closer we got to my departure for Governor's School, the stranger she began to behave.

Outside a Victoria's Secret, our last afternoon together, my mom and I watched two underpaid teens undress and disassemble a mannequin. As the mannequin came apart, her face squeezed in on itself and she lay down across a bench in the mall, hands inked with mascara. I sat with her hand in my lap, studying the black cracks through her palms. Meanwhile the teens brought out another mannequin, which looked exactly like the old one, except its head now faced in the opposite direction.

On a Saturday in June I packed my life into a suitcase and rode to the Governor's School for new student registration. My dad mandated that my mom and I go it alone. Although the drive would take less than an hour, I feared that in her state of mind she'd drive us head on into a train or off the side of a mountain.

My dad woke us up early so we could all leave at the same time. Over a quick breakfast he quizzed my mom to make sure she was road-worthy.

"One last time, you've got the directions. Right? I just saw you put the road map in your purse. You've got my phone number."

My mom placed a hand on mine and whispered to me as if I were embarrassing her. "Sarah, you'd better put some salt on that."

My spoon fell into my cereal. "Okay," I said and reached for the sugar, thinking she wouldn't know the difference.

But she did and her eyebrows dove down. She sat back and folded her arms. "Well, that's going to cost you big time. But not until you least expect it."

My dad knocked on the table. "Monday, listen. Where are you going?"

She mocked him, knocking on the table harder. "Beats the hell out of me. I have a mind to go back to sleep."

"It's simple," he said. "You're going to the Governor's School. You've got directions. Sarah can help if something goes wrong. You've both got my number. Now I've got to head out. I'm almost late. You guys need to leave right after breakfast."

"We're not leaving until Sarah salts her cereal."

His head leaned to one side and for a minute I hoped he would call it off and have her dragged to the hospital. Instead he turned to me. "Sarah, salt your cereal and finish up."

So there we were, me and my mom, stalled in the driveway because she didn't know which way to go. A UPS truck rolled by. "Follow the trucks," she said. "That's what we'll do. They always know where they're going."

My hands covered my face. "Mom, they're all going to different places."

"You're right. We'll have to find a truck with White House license plates."

"What?"

She slapped her thighs. "We're going to the President's School for Fine Arts, aren't we?"

I wanted to punch my dad. He knew she'd been acting weird again, hiding light bulbs in the freezer, painting on the walls. She'd driven to the grocery store and returned with seventeen bags of coffee.

Half an hour placed us somewhere outside Atlanta, skyline just visible over a shelf of trees in the distance. My mom followed trucks at random—delivery trucks and sixteen wheelers. For an hour or two she followed a truck from the steel mill on its way to some unknown construction site. When we crossed into Alabama I sat with my hands wrestling each other. "Mom," I said. "I've got to use the bathroom."

"Piss your pants," she said. "Nobody's watching but me. And we're way late for your doctor's appointment."

"Mom," I said. "We're not going to the doctor."

We looped through Birmingham, her hometown. She pointed out landmarks like a trailer park where she'd taken her first date for a walk after a Hitchcock film, a set of bleachers where she'd killed her virginity, a city square pharmacy where she'd sketched strangers for five cents a picture. The place had faced the courthouse and Sheriff's office, so my mom also drew the hillbilly brawlers and occasional protestor dragged up the stairs for pseudo-justice. We rejoined the highway after a tour of the University of Alabama-Birmingham campus, where she'd said she had made love to a man many times and got pregnant twice and lost the babies. Of course, I didn't know if this was a real memory or another spark of insanity. As if she'd told me a folk tale I wanted to believe.

Our road trip guzzled the last quarter tank. On the state border between Alabama and Mississippi, she finally pulled off at a gas station and cried. "I don't know where we are," she admitted.

At a Mississippi gas station, two scared females in a car are like worms on a hook. I didn't have to have a deep knowledge of the region to spook at the sight of rusted nozzles and dirt-coated windows with browned screens. A man in a blue shirt stared at us. "Ya'll want unleaded?"

I searched the grimed shelves inside for food, finding nothing but ten brands of pork rinds and jerky. As I handed the blue shirt our gas money, a bearded goliath put his hand on my shoulder. "Now what's a-you doing all the way out here, city girl?"

"Going to visit my grandma." How I managed to smile, I can't remember.

Goliath put both arms over his head and giggled. "Shit, grandmas love me. They just love me to death, if you want some company."

I picked up a bag of potato chips and held it against me, like a shield or a stuffed animal. I smiled bigger, stepping back toward the door. Maybe I was thinking about my picture in the newspapers and how sweet I'd look on the missing person flyers they send out in the mail.

Goliath waved goodbye with his fingers.

"You got to pay for them chips now," blue shirt said.

"Shit, I'll buy that little angel a bag of chips any day of the week." And by the time he laid down the two quarters or whatever, I was pumping the hell out of some gas. I prayed neither blue shirt nor Goliath would spot my mom.

I hung up the nozzle and asked her if she could still drive. At fifteen, I'd rarely held a steering wheel for more than a minute. I wondered at what point a minor drives more safely than a maniac.

She pulled out and zipped through back roads. "Used to drive here all the time when I was young," she said. "I know this area. I can get us back to the highway in less than a day."

By then half the Govies had probably unloaded their cars and bid their parents goodbye for the summer. I just wanted to reach a city of some kind and call my dad. He wouldn't comfort me in my crisis, but he'd know what to do.

When we turned down a half-paved landing strip of pebbles I recognized the scenery. We'd taken this road to my grandpa's funeral seven years ago. None of us had forgotten the long downhill spiral of that drive, a perfect match between reality and metaphor—then and now. I'd pasted my forehead to the window, keeping an eye out for brazen deer. I kept thinking we'd passed the same caved-in barn and stable five or six times, but they'd been different enough in their decay. The few things I remember about my grandpa's funeral were the badly dressed families who'd come, the flashes of Polaroid cameras as everyone took final photographs with Gramps in his casket, as if we were at Six Flags, and the fatty fried chicken.

All that fun, seven years ago. Now my mom had come back, like a boomerang. Our car stopped on a plain of gravel that butted up against the country graveyard. A shack of a church stood hip high off the ground, its corners resting on boulders. Her dad's grave was somewhere in the middle of the cemetery. As I remembered, the headstone had been carved out of brick, shaped like a pyramid. Everyone had wanted something original.

My mom drove our car through the graveyard, right up to my grandpa's plot. That's where she backed up the car in a straight line, the pyramid headstone centered in our windshield. She revved her engine. The hood growled and howled, full of wolves.

"Mom, what are you doing?"

"Running over your father's grave."

"Mom, that's *your* dad's grave, not mine."

"It's yours," she said. "I'm trying to do you a favor, Mom. I know you hate that pyramid."

"Why are calling me that? Stop."

"You're Monday West, and that's your dad's fucking ugly head-stone."

I shouldn't have played along, but I did. "Sarah?"

She nodded. "I'm doing this for you, Mom."

Fine. I was her, she was me. The idea worked on some levels. I would become her soon enough, anyway. Why not get a head start?

"Hold on," I said. "Aren't you a little ... tired?"

"Yes, Mom. Exhausted."

"We should take a nap. I mean, we need to rest. We don't want to miss and hit anyone else's headstone. We want our aim to be accurate. Don't we?"

Her eyes closed once, twice. Her grip on the steering wheel loosened. "I guess."

"Just drive back to the church. We'll sleep in the sun. Nice and warm. Okay?"

In the church parking lot, she crawled into the backseat and napped. While she slept I drove through the last of our gas once again, resigning myself to an early death. Unexpectedly we reached a service station, the kind you see in movies. A dirt lot of propane tanks spread out like a mine field. A hard-jawed man in stained overalls wiped our windshield, filled us up, and pen-marked a route on our map. From inside, I could see my mom had woken up. I dashed out to keep her from drinking gasoline at the pump. I found her on her knees, angling the spigot into her mouth. I slapped it out of her hand.

"But it's clear, like water," she said and squeezed the gun, letting unleaded trickle down her fingers. She shut her eyes together and sneezed. Even when she was insane, she was still cute. "I'm so thirsty."

I dragged her to the bathroom and washed her hands over and over.

Before we left, I bought a few bottled waters and duct-taped her wrists together. She'd have to drink from my hand.

"What the fuck is this?" she said. "I'm your mother. You don't handcuff your mother." At least she wasn't me anymore, I thought.

She spoke hate from the backseat across Mississippi, mumbling about friends and loyalty.

In half an hour I'd pretty much mastered basics like steering, gas, and brake. But driving on those dirt roads didn't frighten me half as much as a highway full of cars. An hour of my hell on wheels made me wonder if we wouldn't have been better off with my mom up front anyway. A Luftwaffe of interstate signs and town names flew low over us at the state border between Alabama and Mississippi. I kept wanting to veer off at every exit to be sure it wasn't ours. My foot had little practice in how to ease off on the gas or brakes, so we swung wildly between forty-five and seventy miles per hour. The speedometer looked like a metronome.

The thing about highway patrol cars is that they seem to appear out of the asphalt and mow you down with their blue lights. That's how I got pulled over for the first time in my life, and I screwed that up. Trying to work my way to the emergency lane, I almost sideswiped a Winnebago and then braked too fast. The patrol car squealed to a stop behind us.

"Did we rob a bank or something?" my mom asked. "What's happening? Why have we been pulled over?" She held her head in her hands and rocked back and forth. "Oh, god. What's going to happen to us?"

She tried to pray, and I noticed the duct-tape that still bound her hands. The officer would find this detail peculiar. I shushed her and fumbled through the glove box for something sharp. Scissors. Yes. I leaned into the backseat and grabbed her hands, cutting through the duct tape.

"Please don't hurt me," she said, and cowered.

I held her hands and cut. Soon she was free. I peeled off a few remaining strips of tape.

By the time the officer approached my window, I was shuddering. He asked for my driver's license, and I said I didn't have one, causing him to peer through me to my mom and shake his head. "Ma'am, please step out of the car."

This was it, I was sure. She would do something to get herself arrested or shot. We would spend the night in a Mississippi jail, probably with someone who'd attempted a lynching.

My mom stepped out of the car and addressed the officer politely. I didn't hear everything they said, but their facial expressions, which I studied through the review mirror, persuaded me that somehow my mom had taken back the flight stick of her mind. He still wrote us a hefty ticket, but upon merging back onto the highway my mom was composed and I was in the backseat, ready for sleep.

"Do you know where we are?" I said.

"We need to take this interstate straight back to Georgia and then take 85," she said. "We'll be home before eight or so."

"Are you okay?"

"I'm fine. You know, I found an old sketchbook of yours back there and flipped through it. You draw some weird shit, Sarah."

The sketchbook lay on the floorboard. I yanked it up and studied the drawings I'd forgotten about, charcoal imitations of the sketches the crazy girl had made during my mom's first hospital visit. There it was, the sculptress twisting off her arm and ready to slap it onto the torso of her clay twin.

For half an hour or more I tried reading license plate numbers to keep myself awake, in case my mom got us lost again. But judging from her grip on the wheel and the way she kept glancing at me in the rearview mirror, I decided to trust her.

MY DAD SMOKED an extra pack of cigarettes when we returned. He accused me of being passive. He asked why I didn't stop her from driving to Mississippi. I didn't ask him why he let her go in the first place. I didn't do anything but apologize.

That night we tried to talk her into taking her pills. I sat at the table. What I wanted to say was, hell, if I were my mom I wouldn't want to take the pills either, just to piss him off.

After he called her a loony the fourth time under his breath, she broke the coffee pot on the floor and swallowed all of the pills. She gulped them down with already opened wine. The way our eyes widened, the way we rushed toward the phone ... I wondered if we hadn't been trying to provoke her into slapping someone, shoving someone into a wall, or attempting suicide. It was the only way we could convince the police to take us seriously. Either she took her pills or did something worth their attention, at which point they came and cuffed and loaded her into the back of an ambulance that flashed like Christmas lights.

My dad transported me to Governor's School very late that night. Most of the campus buildings were dark, and my dad wanted to be on his way to bed as soon as possible. We didn't bother to unload half of my things. We hunted down a camp coordinator for my room key, then my dad extinguished his cigarette in a potted plant and pulled an envelope of cash from his jacket.

"Here," he said. "Get whatever you need from the store tomorrow."

"My clothes," I said. "They're in the back, in a duffle bag."

"Oh, all right." Too tired to move, he sighed and popped the trunk for me. I grabbed the bag and almost cried at the idea of leaving behind the bedding, magazines, electric fan, sodas, snacks, and cassettes I'd packed.

My roommate was taking a shower when I dragged my bag through the door. Sketches of Kafka matted one wall. Her closet held nothing but a dozen black sweaters and cotton pants.

Suddenly she stood behind me, wrapped in towels like a patchwork mummy. "Oh, it's you," the girl said. She'd covered most of her face as well. Her hair flowed down like the wings of a sitting crow. From her voice and general appearance I realized to my surprise that she was the asylum girl, whom my mom had befriended and mistaken for me. We didn't look much alike, though we fit the same description. Medium height with dark brown hair. Dark eyes. A little pale and thin.

"How are things?" she asked. "My name's Nera. I remember you, all right, and your mom. Does she still try to set stuff on fire? She did that when she tried to escape one night. Lit up our healing group's piñata project and stashed it under a smoke detector."

"You're pretty talkative for a maniac," I said.

"It didn't start much of a fire. Just sat there, shriveling and smoldering."

"How far did she get?" I said. "At least outside the door?"

"She actually made it to a gas station a few blocks away. A clerk phoned her in because she stripped down and climbed inside one of the coolers to 'chill out.'"

My dad must've kept that story a secret. "I guess you got to know her pretty well."

"I'm not that crazy, by the way. I just get tired of being alive some-times. This is, like, my tenth time as a human. I keep telling them I want to come back as a starfish." Nera undid her towels and dressed, using the bathroom door as a shield. "Look at my doll collection if you want," she said. "They're in the drawers."

Two of them, Barbies. A wind up gear protruded from their backs. Wondering if it was just for looks, I cranked up the blond and planted her on the table. She hobbled several steps before falling onto her stomach. When I cranked up the brunette, she sat quietly for a few seconds. Then she exploded in a fire of springs and gears.

"Shit," I said. "What did I do?"

Nera laughed once. "It's supposed to do that. My mom made them before she left me here. She makes cuckoo clocks and watches and things like that. My parents own a whole company. What do your parents do, besides go crazy I mean?"

"My dad runs an art gallery." On my hands and knees I searched for body parts and springs, wondering if this doll could fly apart mul-tiple times or if this was a one-time toy, like a firecracker.

"Runs or owns?"

"Both."

"Is the art any good?"

"He sells Picassos. Nera, I'm going to put the doll back together and probably go to sleep. Is that okay?"

"As long as you don't turn the lights out. I plan on staying up. And by the way. If you're wondering why I was in the hospital with your mom, it's no big deal. I had an eating disorder and some other things. Such as, okay, they found marks on my hip, and you prob-ably can guess the rest. If you think this is some school for the gifted you're only partially right. They put us in here also because we can't take the real world. That's what our parents really think. Every last one of them. This is an asylum. It's just that the kids don't throw up or have bad dreams about men cutting them up and feeding them to goats. Or if they do then they can paint or write or sing about it."

"You've been here a day. How do you know?"

She looked at me, the green in her eyes daggering through her black hair. "You think you're not crazy."

I shrugged, discovering that the brunette's head screwed back on like a toothpaste cap, or a light bulb. "Well. I just don't ... "

"You look a lot like your mom. I bet you take after her. Have you ever thought about mental illness in your family? I bet you've got some suicides and probably some stuff you'll never ever know about. Stuff so bad your whole family keeps it a secret. They're afraid for you."

I whispered, "They hope I won't turn out, you know."

Nera took the Barbie and a tube of red paint from her desk drawer. She inserted it into the doll's mouth and squeezed. "Like her? You probably will. My doctors say I'm not crazy or anything. I just need to focus and meditate and not worry about my self-image. But I heard them talk to your mom, and I heard the nurses and doctors talking in the lounges. Your mom scared the hell out of everyone there. I'm just lucky she was nice to me."

"It couldn't have been that bad. What'd she do?"

Nera wound up the Barbie and tossed her soft-ball style. "Night, Sarah."

I caught the Barbie and threw her in a trash bin, where she super-novaed. Red splattered up the wall.

I lay in bed, reading until I nodded off. I woke up near daylight and saw that Nera had passed out, forming a kind of heap on the floor. For all I knew, she'd gone to sleep there on purpose and would do so the rest of the summer. The girl was that weird. As she mouthed nonsense from a nightmare, I dredged the trashcan containing Barbie's bloody parts and rebuilt her. She didn't look quite right, even after

I'd sponged off the ketchup. Her head connected to her neck at a strange angle, leaving a tiny crevice there that made her look like the victim of a violent crime. That was Barbie for you. Do whatever you want. Kill her and she'll keep her smile, as if for a photographer who would never come. Giacometti might've been pleased.

BREAKFAST TORTURED ME the next morning. A dozen people asked me the same four questions. They wanted to know my name, where I was from, if I knew anyone here, and if I was having a good time so far. When Sharon or Callie or Isabel introduced themselves, they babbled the same information. Finally, we listened to a welcoming speech from the program's headmaster. Then we shuffled off to class, where I met Mr. Nicolas Anjalu for the first time. He arrived fifteen minutes late, dressed in checkered pants, shirt, coat, tie, and top hat. All silk. He wore white-rimmed eyeglasses with shaded lenses that hid his eyes. He dragged a cart behind him with seven or eight rolls of slides stacked atop a projector.

Before greeting us, Mr. Anjalu dramatically slapped his forehead and stomped his foot. "I forget my chalk. Crapola! Oh, well. That is okay. I will do somehow today without it, and make note for next time."

He sucked in some air, absorbing half the oxygen in the room. "Okay, we open our books to page five."

We did, then sat waiting as he skimmed a few pages of the first chapter. His head shook with increasing violence as he read. We leaned forward in an effort to hear the fragments of words and sentences that floated from his mouth, as if we could blow them up like pool toys for a larger meaning. Finally, he slammed the book shut and stood back with the thick book in one hand, lifting his leg the way a pitcher does in baseball, and chucked the book through a window.

Mr. Anjalu then clapped his hands. "That's not the book I was into using. I did not order that book, which inhales. I mean, siphons. You know what I mean."

A student raised her hand and volunteered some clarification. "You mean, the book *sucks*?"

"Ah, yes! A beautiful word! So, how is it, James Dean and French Fries. So American! And I love your flag!"

We laughed. For me, at least, this was the first time a teacher had made me laugh—on purpose.

"Okay, so you draw me a picture now." He paced once up and down the front of the class. We opened our sketchbooks, but as soon as charcoal touched paper he threw up a hand. "Wait, not yet. I'm changing mind. A better idea has entered me, into me, up here in the head. You know what I mean. I want that you all will try to guess my favorite painter."

A thin boy—almost as thin as me or Nera—flirted with the notion of raising his hand and Mr. Anjalu caught him.

"Yes, you. Goth Child. It is all right that I call you Goth Child?"

"My name's Blake, actually."

"Goth Child it is. Now, you will know my favorite painter?"

"Vermeer?"

Mr. Anjalu's face squeezed like a sponge. "No way, Jose! Next. You, with the hair like that of Goldie Locks. I will call you Goldie."

"Can you call me Jessica?"

"You know what I mean, and now what is my favorite painter?"

"John Singer Sargent?"

"Outrageous! Go back to your backwater, John Singer Sargent. Give me break. Next."

I blushed. Others sank down in their seats, fearing their fate. I said, "You."

Mr. Anjalu fell against the chalk board. "Say again?"

"I think you are your favorite painter."

Someone snickered.

"Shut up," he said, and eased his glasses up his nose with a finger. "Why should I not ask you to leave my class for trying to paint me into a narcolepsies. A narccissian? Why I should not say you are the most ridiculous thing I have heard ever?"

"Because I'm right?"

A quiet second.

"Yes," he said, "you have answer. And I will show you all tomorrow my paintings. Now, we dismiss class. It is enough, a good start we did. Have a good day."

I looked at my watch. "We have more than two hours before lunch."

Already with his hand on the door he said, "Draw is your assignment. Everyone draw for these hours and show me after food time. It is also your homework. At one past noon we will do a showing tell. You know what I mean. Bye-bye."

MOST OF THE CLASS LEFT for their dorm rooms, some of us stayed to draw. After lunch, we reconvened and revealed the rotten fruit of our efforts. Mr. Anjalu lounged in the back with a heavy-duty water gun, drenching those who performed below his standards. One girl presented a charcoal kitten. Mr. Anjalu laughed. "But the legs are so long, and the head is so itsy bitsy. Like you. Nice sticks, little head! Next."

The boy Mr. Anjalu had dubbed Goth Child stood up. He held his sketch at his chest. Suddenly, I saw everyone looking at me.

"Holy mother country." Mr. Anjalu fired his water gun at the ceiling. "Goth Child has a crush on the skinny girl in the corner." He smiled at me.

I scowled. "I think the eyes are a little big. And, to be blunt, I'm not sure Goth Child has given much thought to unity or balance. Or proportion. Or anything. I'm not even sure where the focal point is." The pale boy cringed as I slid from my desk and moved closer. My hands danced over his version of me on paper to visualize my critique. "I can't tell what direction the light comes from. I look like I might be sitting outside, but then my face looks like a cop's shining a lamp at me or something."

Mr. Anjalu slapped his knee. "Good, continue. What about balance and movement, you say?"

"I look as if I were sleeping with my eyes open," I said. "Very little emotion on my face. The way I'm sitting, too, the sketch makes me look like a plastic doll."

"You are correct," Mr. Anjalu said. "Goth Child's work is much exaggerated, for you are cute but you are no doll. You two kissy-kissy later." He smiled at Goth Child. "Hey, maybe she show you how to draw later? You know what I mean. I see these things. I bet ten American dollars. Next."

I stood, showing the class what I'd devoted myself to all morning. Oohs and ahs. People covered their mouths, eyes swiveling toward Mr. Anjalu, whose face fell. I had drawn him. He snatched the charcoal from my hands, trembling. "We shall converse after class."

For two hours our teacher ordered us to draw fruit, animals, stones, chairs, ourselves, and each other. He threw a nugget of chalk at one girl for making an apple too round. "Do you ever see perfectly round apple?" he said, pelting her with another piece. "Maybe you find one and show me." We finished ten minutes early, and I hoped to sneak out without catching Mr. Anjalu's attention. But he hooked me by the collar with his index finger and pulled me toward the desk. Sweat dampened the hair at my neck. My armpits and elbows were slick.

Mr. Anjalu placed his hands on his hips. "I have questions for you," he said, looking into his sketch. "You go very harsh on Goth Child. You can dish out what you plate?"

"You mean, take what I dish out?"

"You know what I mean."

My shoulder rubbed against Mr. Anjalu's elbow as we critiqued my work. I had drawn him in mid-gesture, one hand thrown out toward the class. "You see class from behind, but you see all the little heads snap back. Surprise! And with other hand I pull at my belt." He squinted. Then nearly pressed the sketch to his glasses as he paced about the room. He nearly tripped over my feet, but I caught his shoulders and steadied him.

Mr. Anjalu's fingers tapped the surface of the sketch. "Oh, but here you make big mistake." He waved at the walls. "Measurement is off. Sketch stretches room too skinny. Everything face wrong way." He cackled.

"I did that on purpose."

"Why?"

"Emphasis," I said. "Your finger should jab into the viewers' eyes, so I skewed the room. I turned our class into more of a corridor, which is kind of how being in class with you feels."

Mr. Anjalu flapped the sketch before my face. "So how you feel about room change reality of room. This you say to me?"

I nodded.

I waited to see what he would do. His hands tugged at the edge of my sketch, as if he might tear my drawing in half.

"Very clever. You must have private teacher, yes?"

"My mom paints." I hugged my arms. "She's like you, I guess."

He nodded. "Does she have sister? That is joke. You are best student I know in group. Don't let felines out of canisters, okay? You know what I mean."

"Thanks, Mr. Anjalu."

He stopped me before I could gather my pad and pencils, which had spilled into a heap in my chair. "I have final request," he said. "Go to have this framed and bring tomorrow. I hang this in special place."

"Your office?"

"No, silly. Across from toilet in home bathroom."

MR. ANJALU'S CLASS became my sole occupation. I skipped all of the school's other activities, such as dinner and evening socials. I spent all my free time drawing. Once or twice, however, I found distractions in the library, reading about schizophrenia and how many artists suffered (or flourished) under the spell of mental illness. They wrote wonderful poems about their states of mind before shoving their heads in ovens or dying in back alleys from consumption. In some cases, they completed a new painting every day for months on end, and then one bleak hour walked into a cornfield with a shotgun—never to return. I also learned that you're a good deal more likely to suffer mental breakdowns if one parent carries the magic schizophrenic gene. If both parents suffer, your odds space-shuttle up the chart of vulnerability. Somewhere in cyberspace I found a mental health statistics website, along with an emotional illness calculator. Plug in your crazies: cousin, second cousin, sister, grandparent. The calculator spat back your statistical vulnerability. Your probability of mental illness is about thirty percent higher than the average person's. Plug in both parents and a sibling. Probability is around seventy percent higher than normal.

What that meant: if both parents possess the pixie dust, then you're pretty much fucked.

While my friends played soccer or baseball in the late afternoons, I toyed with my mental illness calculator. Math posed a challenge for me, but I figured out its algorithms—how to add and multiply and divide my mental-emotional future. I also developed an interest in hypotheticals. Take someone with a great-great-grandparent and a cousin, both schizophrenic. If that person marries into the circle of the mentally ill, then his or her risk of producing schizophrenic offspring looks the same as it would for someone with an insane brother and grandparent. Someone with a crazy uncle suffers the same risk as someone with two aunts. My math is terrible, so I could be wrong.

These charts and accessories come heavily armed with disclaimers and advice. Avoid stress. See a counselor. Stay away from caffeine and other mood de-stabilizers, such as alcohol.

Something like seventy percent of schizophrenics tend to smoke. They shouldn't.

Join a support group.

Once, I got a real jolt. The intercom in my classroom crackled to life and asked Mr. Anjalu to send me to the office. I packed my books and paced up front, wondering who was waiting.

My dad?

My mom?

A cop?

Neither. It was a social worker. She wanted to know the details of my road trip with dear old mum earlier that week. Some secretaries cleared out of a small office in the back to give us privacy. We began with preliminary questions.

"Everything's fine," I said, and tried hard to smile. "I mean, my mom acts polite most of the time. She got a little confused earlier."

The social worker apologized as she opened a leather folder. She had to ask me a series of standardized questions before we got to that particular incident.

"Does your mom hit you?"

"Could you define hit?" I said.

"That typically counts as a yes."

"Sorry. I was just trying to be difficult. No, she doesn't."

"Does she use abusive language or raise her voice? If so, rate it on a scale of one to ten."

"No bad language. If she raises her voice, it's a six or seven." Lie. "I mean, that's if five is normal and one is a whisper."

Questions came and went. I walked a line. I had to be careful with my answers. Too bad, and she would come to visit more often. Too good, and she'd get suspicious. I resented the whole process. Standardized questions got standardized answers.

"On a scale of one to ten, rate the sanitation of your house."

"I don't know. Eight. My dad does most of the cleaning."

"Now, tell me about that drive?"

"Can I ask *you* a question?"

Her eyes narrowed. She repositioned her necklace. "That depends, Sarah."

"Is Mom okay? Where is she? Sorry, I know that's two questions. But they're related."

The social worker crossed her legs and re-crossed them, then pulled at her skirt. My mom, she said, was currently seeking treatment at a health center in downtown Marietta. My dad had filed paperwork for a permanent court order that would force her to take medication on a regular basis, enforceable with fines and jail time if she failed to honor the judge's decision. What this meant: my mom would act like a normal person, or she would not be allowed in our house.

I orgasmed stories. "Oh, she shouts so loud my eardrums pop, and she hits me all the time. She's very, very dangerous. A threat to herself and others without a doubt. That trip was horrible, and she got so lost. I was terrified and she made me drive the car halfway home even though I'm only fifteen and she hits Dad, too. And I'm very, very afraid when I come home in the afternoons because she's a brilliant artist but she has a huge temper and sometimes I feel like I should just lock myself up in the bathroom and sleep in the tub because who knows what she's capable of. Once she tried to light my mattress on fire."

The social worker's pen ran laps across her legal pad. After ten minutes she said that was great. She appreciated my help. Have a pleasant afternoon.

That night I hunched over the small desk in my dorm room, determined to repair the windup Barbie and straighten her crooked gait. I poked around in her clockwork insides for two hours. Meanwhile, my roommate stacked furniture on the top bunk so she could paint parodies of the Sistine Chapel on the ceiling.

We stayed up most of the night, committed to silence. The vending machine at the end of our hall became our best friend. Five diet sodas later, I'd tried everything from strings to rubber bands to restore Barbie's sexy strut. Finally, I bent a paperclip into a makeshift hip socket, glued her torso shut extra tight, and wound her up. She cat-walked into Nera's alarm clock and tumbled over, legs kicking. When she wound down I tied her black hair in a bun and propped the doll in a corner. Success. If only every woman were that easy to fix, I thought, while slipping into a wine-stained set of my mom's PJs. The world would need fewer social workers and court orders.

As I drifted off, I heard Nera talking—presumably in her sleep. Then she spoke more clearly, and I knew she was addressing me. "Better ditch that sweat shirt you had on today," she said.

"What are you talking about?"

She chuckled. "Well, I heard a bunch of boys talking about you. They like your knockers. Have any idea what knockers are?"

"I think I catch your drift," I said.

Nera's laughter rose in volume. Our bunk beds rocked to the rhythm of her merriment. The girls next door to us began to bang on the wall. I sandwiched my head between two pillows and waited for everything to end.

The Govy School library owned one documentary on mental illnesses. I checked out the video and watched it in my room while Nera was off somewhere praying to Norse gods. My education began with a skit acted out by Hollywood types. Scene one opened in a bar. In walked a beautiful scarved woman as the narrator said, "Jane was feeling phenomenal after a long day at the office. She'd worked hard for weeks on a big project, and now felt relieved." Jane crossed her legs at the bar, hit on the bus boy, the bartender, and a waitress. Then she ran out to her car and drove it off a cliff.

The narrator's voice broke in at various points to tell me that "Women like Jane sometimes act very promiscuous," or "Women like Jane often get upset for no apparent reason." At the end of the clip, Jane woke up in a hospital bed with her arm in a sling. The doctor began to speak to Jane, and he spoke to her in the voice of the narrator. We found out that, all along, the narrator had been the doctor. He folded his hands behind his back and said, "Jane, you've apparently suffered another manic-depressive episode. Have you been taking your medicine as prescribed by your physician?" The doctor looked a little like my dad. Jane smiled sheepishly. She was so cute you wanted to kiss her.

MY FOUR WEEKS at Governor's School passed too quickly, and I dreaded that hour when my parents would reclaim me. On the last day, Mr. Anjalu showed us slides. We presented final projects. Goth Child finally earned lukewarm praise for his art. He had continued to draw me for most of the month. He had followed me to coffee shops and book stores, to the park, to the library. We'd exchanged only a few words. In the final portrait of me that Goth Child showed our class, I faced the viewer, pencil in hand, as if I were drawing him draw me. Returning to his seat, he placed the work face down on my desk. "Thanks for being my muse," he said.

Only recently had I suspected that I had something to offer the opposite sex. I failed to voice a response. I simply slipped the drawing into my sketchbook.

For my final project, I'd drawn a mug facing an empty pitcher. The seeds of my thesis. Mr. Anjalu said nothing except, "Good as usual. Thank you, little one. You may sit." He reminded me of my dad then, eyes aimed at his fingernails, which he picked with a painting knife.

At three o'clock, students lifted their bags onto their shoulders and strolled back to their dorms, trying to capture the final minutes on film. The hallway had turned into a press conference, practically. Crowds clotted the doorways. Cameras flashed. A quarter past three. My book bag weighed heavily on my shoulders. My parents would arrive at five. As I hit the stairwell, a hand gripped my shoulder. "Not so fast, little one. We must have talk."

Something in Mr. Anjalu's voice struck me. He sounded nice, almost warm. "I have gift."

I followed him back to the classroom. Heat gathered in my chest and spread to my face, then down my stomach.

The door to the classroom closed.

Mr. Anjalu reached into his bag and presented me with a complete set of drawing pencils. "I order them from best company," he said.

I hugged them. "I don't want to go home," I said. I leaned against the chalkboard. White dust smudged my sleeve.

"Of course, you don't. No one ever want to go home after four weeks with Nicolas." He smiled. "But where else you go? Home with teacher? Give me break."

I shivered.

Mr. Anjalu removed his glasses. "Something you don't tell me. What? Your parents make you sweep chimney?"

So I explained things to him.

When I finished, I noticed we had moved quite close. His finger smudged my mascara. Mr. Anjalu pinched his finger and thumb together and squinted, as if studying a strange substance. When had I started treating my face like an art project? I suddenly became aware of my age. I was no child anymore. Mr. Anjalu's finger skimmed across my bottom lip. Who knows what might have transpired if someone hadn't knocked on our door. Who but my mom would have wanted to meet the teacher?

She swept into the room and stopped dead, as if she'd walked into a brick wall. "Well, hello."

"You are the Monday West I hear about?" Mr. Anjalu hopped off his stool. Instantly, I knew everything I'd confessed to him about my mom had been erased and painted over by her stunning image.

My mom's hand touched her hair. "Sarah never told me her art teacher was . . . a . . . "

I folded my arms and huffed. "A handsome Eastern European?"

My mom gasped. "Exactly."

I raised my voice and spoke with extra slow cadence. "So, how was the hospital? Did they give you some new pills?"

They both ignored me. My mom waltzed into Mr. Anjalu's arms and gave him a squeeze. As they chatted, I stood and moved to the door. By the end of their meeting, they'd exchanged cards and kisses on the cheek.

AFTER MY SUMMER OF HAPPINESS, I returned home and continued public high school as usual. A social worker toured our house every month and then told my mom to go upstairs while she asked me questions. My mom and I argued all the time, always about my secret phone conversations with my dad or about her pills. By senior year we lived by ourselves, my dad having left for Columbia three weeks before the first day of class. My mom had slapped me once, and I'd slapped her. I didn't know if that was worth mentioning to the DSS. I didn't want to talk about all of the wine, or my mom's raids into my bedroom at night. My face had gotten good at holding steady, so I didn't have to fake smile or sugar talk. "Okay," I said.

"Has any violence occurred in the past three months?"

"Not really."

"Can you be more specific?"

"Nothing physical. We argue sometimes."

I imagined her leaving any minute, slapping shut her leather notebook and prancing out for good. I hoped my mom would keep her yarn, that she wouldn't come downstairs naked or threaten this woman with a can opener. The women didn't belong here. Other people needed social workers, not me. All I needed was a phone and a good pair of running shoes.

Not much happened the first few weeks of that last year. I came and went, and so did my mom. Once or twice we tried bonding.

But our relationship changed forever when I brought a boy over for dinner. His name was Rob, and he drew cartoons for the school newspaper. He had curly hair and a decent sense of humor. I remember he had been the one to suggest meeting my parents after we'd spent a few minutes on his bed one afternoon. The night he came, my mom ordered Chinese. We ate from boxes, with chopsticks.

My mom was in rare form. She caused great mischief with her chopsticks, snapping at us playfully between bites. When Rob took the last mini-egg roll my mom pinched his nose. "So, Rob, I'm always looking for models. I used to draw Sarah." She smiled at me, mock innocence agleam in her green eyes, showing her teeth. "But she seems so distant these days. I miss it, our sessions together."

Rob nodded, eyes almost cross-eyed as he glanced toward his nose, still caught in her chopsticks. He sneezed.

My mom grimaced and switched to a fork. "I drew her nude, you know. She has a very nice body. But, of course, I'm sure that's not news to you."

My face warmed. "Mom, Rob doesn't need to know that."

"She draws me nude, too. Used to, I should say. What do you think about that, Rob? Does it turn you on? I'm just curious. In some ways, I'm a sociologist. I'm very interested in the dynamics of sexual attraction." She scavenged Rob's plate, skewering a carrot as she shot him a wicked smirk. Her tongue slithered out to lick the orange surface.

I pulled Rob's plate out of her reach. "Mom, please."

She raised her wine glass. "It's always hard to tell if your daughter's slept with the boy she brings over. But, either way, I'm guessing you'd like to see those nudes. Nobody understands a girl's form like her mother." Her hand crept across the table over to his. "I could draw you, too. You and Sarah together. An evening you'll never forget."

"Mom!"

She moved to the dining room wall with a marker in hand. "Here, let's set a date. I'll keep that appointment right where I can see it."

I latched my hands on my mom's wrist and pulled her into the living room. I begged her to stop, then threatened. She told me to lighten up. When we returned to the table, Rob had left. A surprise attack of wind shoved open the door. I dashed to the porch and caught the sinking glow of headlights as a car rolled down the street and made a sharp right.

I leaned against the doorframe, hiding my face.

My mom's fingers ploughed into my hair. She kissed my forehead, cheeks. "It's okay," she said. "Let me guess. You hadn't even kissed that boy yet. I'm sorry. I'm sorry he did that."

"I had."

She tried to hug me. I pushed her back. She stumbled through the foyer and clung to the banister. She was clearly still foggy-headed from the wine. As I charged toward her, she crab-walked up the stairs. For years I'd been terrified of her. Now it was payback time.

"No," she said. "Calm down."

"Do you know what you did," I yelled. "You do this all the time. You never know when to shut up. You're so fucking stupid."

Dragging her to her knees by the collar of her blouse, I slapped her, just once, but so hard my palm numbed. The slap ricocheted, echoed. It was like someone had shot a firecracker. The numbness spread up my arm. I scoffed at myself, looking at my hand. She cried like seven or eight people at a wake. For eight years of crap, all I needed was one slap. I helped her downstairs and made hot tea and rubbed lotion on her cheek. She kept telling me I was right. She was stupid. She was going to quit the alcohol and start taking her pills every day.

AFTER I'D SLAPPED THE HELL out of my mom, we begin to get along much better. She pulled herself together and, as fortune smirked on us, found a medication that allowed her to focus—which meant she would stay on it for once. Sometime in late autumn, my senior year of high school, she brought her art class out to the diner, where I'd been waiting tables. But I wasn't working that night. She called at home while I was drawing my fifteenth copy of *Woman with her Throat Cut*.

"You thought it'd be fun to what . . . make me wait on you and your friends? I'm trying to draw, Mom. Today's my only day off this week."

She sounded like she might cry. "You're right. I'm, it's okay. I thought you were working, and I just wanted them to meet you. You might've shown them some of your work or something or . . . I don't know. I'm just, okay."

I changed and drove to the diner. In my plaid outfit, I dragged the waitress on duty into the nonsmoking section and asked to have that one table for the night. She could even keep the tips. "Fine with me, honey. They look like they'd tip about as well as a crash test dummy."

They'd shoved a couple of tables together to seat about ten, including my mom, the only one of them even trying to smile. Even I couldn't tell them apart. They all wore thick-rimmed eyeglasses. Some had chosen standard black frames for their eyewear, while others had striven for a more fun-loving intellectual look with red or green frames. Truckers, plumbers, construction men, retired military, and gas station clerks at the other tables stared at my mom's colleagues with big twisted grins. Many of them waved or tipped their fishing caps at me as I walked in. The art geeks flipped their eyes in my direction and looked away, as if they didn't know what to do. My mom had clearly ordered these people here, or begged.

"Crap," I said to myself when I recognized the ambiguously Eastern European man with his hand on my mom's knee—the only one with anything close to a happy face. It was Mr. Anjalu. I didn't know if they'd talked about me. Maybe I shouldn't try to find out.

I distributed menus and kept my head tucked, scribbling down drinks, then retreated to the butler station, where I filled sodas and teas. Free drinks, to make up for the lack of bourbon and wine.

They should've known better.

Most of them took a long time to decide what to order. They looked at their menus like children who'd gotten coal for Christmas.

One of them asked me with a melting frown what okra was. That's when Mr. Anjalu came to my aid.

"You don't know, and how long you have lived here? I come here from another country. First day, I say I'm going to eat every food of this bizarre place. Get the okra, you will like. If not, slide it over here."

"Ya'll want any appetizers?"

"Hello, little one!"

A few of them snickered. My mom blushed and excused herself to the restroom.

I followed her. "I'm doing the best I can."

"What's with the accent, Sarah?"

"I don't know. I just do it here. I get bigger tips."

"Well, I mean. Knock it off."

"Am I embarrassing you?"

"No, yourself. Look, just be you. All right?"

"When did you start dating my art teacher?"

"He's here showing some work at the college, and he's been talking about you all weekend. He wants to direct your thesis project."

"Mom, why didn't you just invite me out?"

"I guess I didn't think of that. I just didn't envision it like that. I thought you could take a short break, you know, and talk with Nic."

"You couldn't picture it, me sitting down with you and your friends. I had to serve them first. Great, worse than Dad."

"That was my goal. Do I win a plaque?"

13

JULY CRAWLED FORWARD. Edgewood continued to paint without detection. My dad and I made further attempts to bond. A week after the Fourth, a special letter arrived. The chair of Emory's art department invited me and the other newcomers to a special lunch in Atlanta. We would eat at a place called Dulahan's, which charged five dollars a glass for its gourmet ice tea and provided a view of the muddy Chattahoochee River. When I asked my dad for that Friday off from work, he nodded yes and told me to try the lobster. "One of my crewmen said they serve the best lobster in the state. I'm not sure why he ordered lobster on his salary, but I'll take his word." He flipped a fifty across the table.

"I'm allowed one guest," I said.

"Really?"

I looked down at the table. "Yeah, if you want to hang out with a bunch of snobs. I mean, it might be fun afterwards. We could stop by the house or the mill."

A finger twirling his mustache, he squinted hard. "You know what you should do? Why don't you visit the Atlanta mill and draw some pictures. I'd like some sketches of the old place."

"I guess that means you'd rather not come."

"Well, I'm busy these days."

Outside, two cats copulated under a dogwood tree near the edge of our back fence. They didn't notice me as I sat on my knees and drew them. After dinner I drove to Edgewood's and found him napping in one of the upstairs jail cells. Bricks lay scattered about the floor, beneath a gaping hole in the wall. Edgewood traced my gaze to the damaged area and explained that, in 1927, the mayor of Columbia had accidentally fired a cannon at the prison during a Civil War reenactment. I looked at the bricks, amazed, wondering if they had really sat there for almost a hundred years. The window sills were spattered with pigeon stool. A cage for two people stood in the room's center, a medieval-looking torture device welded to the bars.

We talked about my upcoming lunch.

"Go with you to Emory?" he said, then looked through the iron crosshairs of the window, at a dead tree.

"You could meet the chair, show him some of your work. You know, if they offered anyone late admission, he could pull strings."

"I'd better not," he said. "I like it here. I'm not ready for art school. But thanks."

As the afternoon passed, I drew Edgewood while he completed a new mural. We worked for hours. After he slapped his hands dry on his jeans and left for a shower, I ripped my sketch of him from my pad and pressed his image against the iron grillwork of a window.

At Dulahan's the art department chair kept staring at me. His name was Hasselbrad Karsiko, and he looked painfully familiar— something about the shape of his eyebrows. I tried to make friends with the other nerds, who shared my social anxieties. But mostly, we listened to Dr. Karsiko's stories and answered his questions. He wouldn't turn his eyes toward anyone else, only me. Something in his face reminded me of someone but I couldn't think who. Then he caught his breath and he blinked. "I know you," he said. "Sarah West. You are student of my cousin, Nic." He scratched at his wasp's nest of messy black hair. "I know your name and stories of your mother. A very charming woman, though I am sorry for the loss of her life."

I shrugged. "How is Mr. Anjalu? I haven't seen him in a while."

"Oh, he is fine. Always painting these days, like me. Or sometimes he is, you know the saying, getting his groove on with some young piece. Yes?"

"Sure, that's great."

As the meal progressed I got to meet some of the other incoming students. For example: Luke had grown up in Kansas, where he photographed prairie dogs for his senior art project in high school.

"How adorable," someone said.

"Actually I photographed the dead ones," he corrected. "We kill them all the time. They cause huge problems with the, um, irrigation systems."

A girl named Kelly Smerk talked about her recent work. She specialized in miniature versions of crop signs. She went to great lengths for detail, making the tiny corn stalks one at a time and then flattening them into alien patterns.

Near dessert, someone pointed at one of Edgewood's prints that I'd brought and asked me to unravel it. "Okay," I said. I showed them an imitation Edgewood had painted of Orozco's *El Martirio de San Estabon*, a gaggle of moon-white ghosts crushing a man to death with boulders.

"You're amazing," Dr. Karsiko said.

I blushed. "It's not my work, actually."

"Whose, then?"

"My boyfriend's."

Dr. Karsiko asked for all three of the prints I'd brought and spread them across the table. They made a canopy over half of our desserts.

People crooned. One guy began to salivate at a busty Mestiza in the background. A hoard of wait staff crowded around. Among the faces at the table, I found Edgewood's.

"Jesus," I said. 'What are you doing here?"

"I noticed the prints gone this morning." He cleared his throat. "You left the door to the storage closet open."

"Are you angry?" I said, standing behind him.

"I don't know. I'm very something."

Dr. Karsiko introduced himself, shook Edgewood's limp and trembling hand, then buried him in compliments. He reddened as they told him to apply. My new friends looked down at the artwork that separated them from their pricey pecan pies. The crop signs girl, on her third glass of Merlot, cried a little. "I suck," she sighed into her hands. "I hate myself. I don't deserve to be here." People on both sides tried to pat her shoulders. I wanted to say something to help her but, really, what could I do? She needed something I wasn't qualified to give.

Meanwhile, Edgewood stared through his appraisers. After a few minutes they realized they were spending too many words on his ego. He didn't seem to care. It was like congratulating a paint brush for its fine job on the Mona Lisa. "Sarah, please do me a favor. Roll them up now and put them away, before someone spills tea on them." Then he turned and strode off.

I stayed to chat, sneaking in an explanation for Edgewood's abrupt and rude departure. Then I left. I imagined all the ways he might react. Dump me and move to another shitty mill town and piss off another plant manager with his murals. Apply to Emory and live with me forever in a somewhat perfect world. Or disappear and leave me wondering.

Ironically, our cars met up on the highway. We got stalled in Atlanta traffic and managed to converse with our windows rolled down.

Edgewood's hand stuck out the car window, cupped as if to catch the wind.

"Stop that," I said. "Put your arm back in the car, before it gets knocked off."

"You sound like my mom."

"That's not the point," I said. "The point is put your arm back in the car."

"You shouldn't have gone with those prints. Not without telling me."

"Better to beg forgiveness, etcetera."

"I don't know if Dr. Karsiko was sincere," Edgewood said. "How am I sure he won't forget who I am? I apply and he forgets. Or, worse. I can't trust that lunch. Now I'll expect something. I'll hope. I hate hoping."

"He won't forget you. I'm going to keep talking about you."

"Don't do that," Edgewood said. "They'll get sick of me."

"Shut up. You're such a whiner. I did you a huge favor and you whine. Thanks."

My car passed under the exit sign to the old plant where my dad had worked. The name brought back memories, and I wondered what had happened to the place. The steel company had been going out of business, dying slowly, for years before my dad left. As captain, he'd practically gone down with the ship. I invited Edgewood to tour its abandoned buildings with me. We pulled off at a service station, where he hopped in my car.

We drove.

"So your dad worked here, you said. I've heard about Atlantic Steel, I think. Huge plant, almost like Bethlehem Steel, went bankrupt for some of the same reasons as Bethlehem. Did they have elevator girls there?"

"No elevators, unfortunately. I'm sure they aspired to have office buildings that tall one day. My dad worked there a long time, twenty years."

"That's tough to imagine," Edgewood said, "working at the same place for that long."

My hands squeezed the steering wheel. "And yet."

"Yeah."

"Do you want to see it? Most of the mill's still there. Maybe it's haunted now."

He said, "Let's go."

Despite its hundreds of acres, the old plant was hard to find. Signs had been taken down. My memory barely did its job. The plant was hidden deep in an industrial slum, surrounded by warehouses. When I'd almost given up on finding our way, I saw a tower of charred steel rising from behind a bundle of tenement apartments. Ah, I thought, the blast furnace. Unmistakable in its rusted grandeur.

The thing was huge, dwarfing nearby buildings.

We used it like the North Star, and eventually found ourselves at the opening of a tall fence. Weeds and grass had returned, working up certain poles. A lawnmower lay on its back, weeds protruding from its insides. Vines wreathed the blades and steering wheel.

We parked in a trash-littered lot and climbed out, sizing up the tall grayed buildings and dead cranes. Scrap sat in enormous piles, like collapsed buildings. Outside the melt shop, we stopped to admire a ladle turned on its side, which sat next to a stack of crumbling manganese bricks.

"You know what my dad did when I told him about Emory? He made a list of all the buildings Atlantic Steel had built on its campus."

Edgewood nodded. He walked a few steps ahead, kicking pieces of rebar and debris out of our path.

"I'm curious," I said. "What about your family? You've kept them a secret, like most things."

"Girls love a puzzle."

"You get a weird look every time I mention your parents. You remember our conversation that one day, when I asked why you weren't looking for scholarships or asking for help from them?"

"Yeah," he said. "I don't know. Does everybody have to talk about family?"

"What, did they die? Were you abused?"

"Were *you*?"

"I see what you're doing. Me is not the point, nor is my mom. Anyway, it was just a question. Forget I said anything."

We walked, taking in the melt shop and rolling mill, thinking about their giant loneliness until it was all we could feel.

He lit cigarettes for us and breathed through his for a few seconds. "You know, my dad used to sneak into my room at night and screw up my paintings. Graffiti, you know. Vandalism, real vandalism. I made art for the high school drama club, sets and stuff. Costumes, like Picasso did for the ballets in Paris." He smirked at his smoke. "My dad couldn't decide if I was wasting my time or showing him up. He taught high school art. He was never that great. He thought I was."

"You are, Edgewood."

He shrugged. "So I moved out. It's not what you'd think. Sleeping in places like this. I stayed with friends, around town. I had jobs and cash. Last I heard, he was fired from the high school for making his students cry. Go figure."

"Well, I'm sorry." I tried to hug him but he walked off. "I'm glad you told me. You wanted to, right? You wanted to open up. Forgive the cliché. It's good. We need to talk about these things. You're right."

He walked. I followed.

"I'm sorry. My mom was about as bad. She, well, she did things similar to that."

He tapped his cigarette out with his foot and took mine. Some of my lip gloss had come off on it. He shrugged and dipped it between his lips.

"So I've been thinking," Edgewood began.

We'd wandered into the shipping warehouse, an open building with train tracks running through it. Train tracks galore spread out before us, cutting lengthwise across the far end. A train bellowed and flowed past, tugging too many railcars to count.

We crunched onto gravel. I tried to find a piece to focus on. "About us," I said and looked up.

Edgewood's eyes squeezed shut and then, striding off, he drop-kicked a rock across the warehouse. The rock clanged against an iron support beam as he rubbed his neck. "We're not working," he sighed.

"God. You're serious," I said. "We can fix this problem, can't we?"

He shook his head.

We spoke in one-word sentences. Slowly, I lost the argument. Losing was like watching a toy ship fill up with water and drop to the bottom of the bathtub. I sat down on the gravel, half-Indian style, and covered my mouth. Then I suddenly felt like cutting something into little pieces. "My mom tried to kill me once," I said. "Beat that."

14

PEOPLE SAID THAT IF YOU DIED in the mill, your spirit stayed behind so it could keep working. I didn't believe them until August, when two crewmen lost their lives. The first worker died when the rolling mill cobbled, something that happened often though usually without death. To understand cobbling, you must understand how rebar is finally made from the endless heaps of rusty scrap that arrive daily and pour into the melt shop, which produces flat boards of metal called billets, which are loaded into the rolling mill like bullets into a handgun. In the rolling mill, the last stage, long rods of bright red steel whizzes through a series of machines called stands. If the stands become misaligned, then the rods kink and buckle, eventually spilling out onto the floor. Anyone caught in the path of these rebellious strips of steel faces terrible danger.

The day of the worker's death, I watched from a safe distance as a red strip of steel flopped out of the fifth stand in lunatic loops and bled across the rolling mill floor. A siren scaled octaves, and emergency lights flashed like cameras at a concert. Workers scrambled out of the mill's darkness and into the sunlight, but one of them fell and must've sprained his ankle. He rose to a hobble. The steel spiraled outward and lassoed him. His face seemed to crack as he felt the searing whips of metal on his flesh. I was puzzled that he didn't scream. If he did, his voice only faded into the deafening noise.

My dad appeared in the entrance to the mill. The rays of sun that blasted through the doorway prevented me from making out the features of his face. Daylight burned the details from everything else. Everyone I saw looked like construction paper cutouts.

In the time it takes an eye to blink, my dad ascended the stairs leading to the control room. I followed him and stood outside, my face pressed to the glass, studying him. He ushered stunned and panic-eyed engineers out of the way and placed himself at center of a solar system of buttons and gauges. His hands hopped across the console. Soon, from every direction, came the sound of death. The prescient hum of electricity fell to a murmur, then ceased altogether. Now I heard nothing, except a family of pigeons that trilled from a corner of the mill's ceiling. I looked to the rolling mill floor. Red continued to squiggle around its victim. The man's body twitched, and twitched, and then sagged. The accident looked like a neon sign, the kind you see outside stores.

A crowd formed by the entrance to the mill and grew like a cancerous cell as steel hoops looped out and outward, slower now, until finally they all turned a darker, deeper red and rigidified. The only visible part of the trapped worker that remained was a limp arm. The rest of him was buried in the twists of steel. Once the steel had cooled into solid gray spirals, men in welding masks carved the dead man out of the hardened twists with blow torches. It was like one of my mom's paintings had come to life.

I didn't know how these welders would cut an organic body out of that steel mess without dismembering him. Edgewood and the others slit the warped rebar away, one strip at a time. Gradually they discovered what remained of him, a mannequin made out of silly putty with deep crimson wounds across his limbs, wounds made and cauterized in the same lightning slashes.

An article about the dead man appeared in the newspaper in the obituary section. A memo circulated around the offices at work, text wrapped around a family photo. He smiled, spatula in one hand, hamburger in the other. So ordinary, I thought. And I'd never seen him before. Or maybe I had, and his hardhat and glasses had concealed his identity.

At his funeral, mill workers filled the right side of the church, family the left side—almost like a wedding. He had two baby daughters, twins. They babbled and cooed and hummed along with the organ music.

HIS DEATH LED TO THE END of my artist's block. The images of his demise kept me awake all night in front of my sketchbook. Half-formed ideas grew into doodles, which my pencil mutated into monstrous visions. I imagined the worst mill accidents, not as my mom would have, but through the macabre eyes of Giacometti. My charcoal sticks burned across page after page. Finally, I drew a skeleton immersed in a sea of razor-thin serpents. I couldn't decide on an angle. I tried several vantage points, but none satisfied me. I needed them all, so over the course of a week I drew blueprints for a series of sculptures. I would not use clay, nor alabaster, nor sand. I would use metal, my new element.

The first Saturday night of August, I entered the steel plant through a side gate. It was a fine night, everything in sight shaded navy blue. A pack of freight trucks loaded down with rebar made a single-file line at the scale house, waiting to be weighed before they cruised off and onto the highway. I drove past them and turned onto a remote gravel road that wrapped around the plant's perimeter, where old warehouses stood. Abandoned long ago, iron roofs rusted and caving in, they provided artifacts from the mill's ancient history. The entire plant had moved gradually west over the last eighty years, leaving behind a trail of forgotten buildings. I drove on. The old roadway was a playground for snakes and hornets, and possibly ghosts.

The scrap yard looked like an elephants' burial ground, bent rebar poking up from the dirt like ribs. I slouched through a forest of cars, forklifts, refrigerators, gears, and pipes, looking for the right spare parts to build my pretty little monsters. I woke the dead and dug them up and hid them under a tarp so the moon couldn't kill them all over again.

A flashlight pinned me down.

I stopped and stared in the direction of the beam, deer-like in my terror.

"What are you doing out here, Sarah?" said the flashlight's owner.

He stepped closer, into the line of the moon's fire.

It was Edgewood.

My eyes narrowed. "Oh, hi. I guess I should've known you'd be out here. Plan on painting tonight? Hope I haven't disturbed your agenda."

His flashlight shined into the pieces of rebar I'd gathered. "What is all that for?"

"New art project," I said.

"Want some help?"

"Well," I said, "I could use your truck."

He parked his truck behind a tower of old tires, then we swung my iron elephant ribs onto the bed.

"Where are we taking this?" he asked.

"To my house," I said. "I want to take these pieces home and figure out how to use them in a sculpture."

"What is your plan?"

"I need to find a way to mold the metal."

"I know an easy way to do that."

"Which is . . . "

"Nobody's using the metallurgy lab right now. They lock the doors at night, but I can get in. I also know how to use the equipment."

"Are you sure?" I said. "Don't you have to paint?"

"I can wait. This idea sounds interesting. I'd like to see how things turn out."

When we reached the lab, I dragged my rebar inside. Some pieces were so heavy they tore gashes into the gravel. I made piles along the lab's walls and then studied my sketches, Shaun's death depicted in a storm of charcoal slashes.

Edgewood warmed up a machine called a bar bender. As he did, I chose my bones: a straight stick of steel for the spine, four gnarled ones for arms and legs, a welding mask for the head. Edgewood wedged the strips of rusted steel bar into the bender. Its iron wheels forged them into limbs.

We lay the body parts together to give ourselves a preview. The victim's mask stared through us—8-millimeter fingers caressing the pythons of steel that pinned him down.

Edgewood fastened a welding mask to my head and clicked on the torch. I knelt at the waist of our victim and touched the flame to the place where tailbone met left leg. Edgewood held everything together as I burned our art into being.

We worked for a long time in silence. Two a.m. surprised us. I stood and flipped up my mask. Before me lay the sculpture I would call *Cobbled*, a nightmare marriage between Edgewood's murals and my mom's paintings.

Edgewood wiped his face with a rag. "What now?"

"Nothing," I said. "Thanks for your help. You should go home and get some rest. I'm sorry I used up your evening."

He tossed his rag onto the bar bender. "Let's go for a walk."

We circled the mill twice, Edgewood pointing at the sides of buildings he'd used for murals. "I must've painted that one ten times," he said, at the south side of the rolling mill. "Every time, someone washed it off." He dug his hands in his jacket pockets and kicked a piece of gravel. "I wonder if anybody misses my murals."

"I do."

At three in the morning we walked to the old warehouses. Edgewood told me which ones were haunted. One warehouse was haunted by a man who'd been skewered by a strip of rebar in 1955. Another warehouse was haunted by a man who fell into a ladle full of lava-hot steel. Others were haunted by workers who had died of everything from thirst to balls of flame. One worker had been sucked into a pit of hot ash by a faulty vent and suffocated. His lungs were full of soot when the medics examined his body. Mills were dangerous places today, but fifty years ago you never knew when someone might be working their last twelve-hour shift on earth. Edgewood and I held hands. A baby deer sprinted across the tracks, from one patch of woods to another.

At around four-thirty, we teased the night shift at the scale house. We stood on the enormous scale and weighed ourselves, but we came in at just over two-hundred and fifty pounds. "You need to gain a few tons," I said.

We should've gone to sleep.

The sky blued. I was starting to feel drunk. I fell into Edgewood. We paused before a heap of rubble. Who knew what the bricks had once been?

When we reached the melt shop, Edgewood stepped closer to me and took off his hardhat, then he took off mine. I took off my safety glasses, then his.

"About the other day," he said, "on the way back from Emory. I didn't mean all of that. I was confused." He held my hardhat, rubbing his thumb along my name. "I want to go with you to school in Atlanta, even if I'm still sort of worried that I might not have what it takes."

We stood close, arms around each other. My chin dug into his collar. My eyes watered, and my eyelashes painted black stripes on the nape of his neck. I didn't tell him how scared I'd been, the thought of leaving him here with my dad indefinitely. Part of me felt ashamed for needing someone as badly as I did. I wished, someday, to be able to pick up and go. Isn't that part of being an artist, for lack of better words?

"Hey, sun's coming up," I said and pointed over his shoulder. "Over there."

The clouds looked blood-soaked and beautiful.

Our stomachs were empty and felt corroded. The sleepless hours had bludgeoned our balance. Every step made us feel as if we were walking a plank. How nice it would've been to climb into bed and sleep. Instead we doused our nerves with coffee, speaking mostly in groans. We shared a biscuit from a vending machine and complained about the awful strung-out day that awaited as punishment for my night of wild inspiration. I urged Edgewood to go home, to call in sick. But he wouldn't. He kissed my cheek and told me to be careful. We parted near the shipping office, and I spent the rest of the morning in my dad's office, shrouded in busywork. On my way to deliver a stack of reports to the payroll office, however, I stopped to watch Edgewood, who knelt at the top of a stack of rebar in the distance. Magnetic cranes hung above the driveway like guillotines.

One of the overhead cranes came sliding across the warehouse with a ten-ton load of rebar. Edgewood knelt, wiping off sweat and trying to keep his eyes open. If I hadn't kept him up so late working on my naïve sculpture project, he surely would've reacted more quickly. The crane operator continued to sound its customary warning siren as he approached, but Edgewood only slumped down Indian-style onto a hot bundle of rebar, head in his hands. I waved and shouted at him, but failed to attract his attention. Perhaps if the crane operator had also concentrated more on his job, the accident could've been avoided. However, simply because the operator sounds his siren, that doesn't mean he sees someone in harm's way. Safety regulations require operators to signal anytime they're carrying steel. The responsibility falls to people on the ground to watch out, for often the operator can't see everyone from his position.

My dad and everyone else had explained many times the danger of standing under the magnetic cranes. Losing power to the magnets was not uncommon, and when that happened the cranes lost their hold on the rebar, which would descend with skull-crushing force. Anyone who chose to ignore an oncoming crane held the responsibility for his own injury should an accident occur.

The cranes rocked forward and dropped their bundles. They avalanched onto Edgewood. My legs melted beneath me. Any seed of a scream was vacuumed from my throat.

Mill workers scrambled for help like pool balls. As crowds gathered, a dozen men barked commands into their CB radios. I stole a pair of welding gloves from someone's back pocket and launched myself onto the stack. Heat washed through my nose and down my throat as I climbed, a sensation that made me feel as if I were drowning. When I reached the top I tried pulling Edgewood out from under the bundle of steel that had smashed into him. His hard hat slipped off and toppled like a pebble down the side of the stack. Realizing the futility of my efforts, I pressed my weight against the bundle. Pushing so hard I thought my bones would fold in on themselves, I felt the bundle give. I shoved again. The bundle seesawed and rolled down the stack and thundered onto the driveway, spilling open like a bag of guts. I vomited on Edgewood's pants. My head drooped into the crook of his knee.

WHEN I CAME TO, I was lying in a hospital bed, my arm in a sling. I didn't try to move, feeling the medicated throb of severed muscles around my shoulder and elbow. My dad's hardhat dangled from a coat rack's arm. A pack of his nicotine gum sat between my feet. I imagined him sitting at the foot of my bed, chewing and wishing for a real smoke and waiting for his daughter to awake.

A physician pulled a chair up to my bed and told me Edgewood was gone. A short silence followed, in which he fiddled with his stethoscope. This doctor looked young, barely out of med school, and I imagined this to be his first time breaking bad news. He wore a beard, maybe to make himself appear older. Or maybe he didn't like the bottom half of his face. I didn't want to trouble this person further, but I asked anyway—to see Edgewood.

The doctor asked me if I was sure I wanted go through with this. I said yes, then I followed him down a corridor to an elevator that took us to a cold hallway. In the third room to the left, I held my head in place as a sheet slid off Edgewood's body. He reminded me of a still life.

I borrowed the physician's stethoscope. I leaned over Edgewood and placed its cold metal against Edgewood's chest. After some amount of time I draped the stethoscope around the physician's neck. I said, "I understand how you could mistake him for dead. But he's just pretending. We stayed up late last night. Now he wants us to leave him alone for a little while so he can rest. You should turn up the temperature a little, or bring him a quilt. It's chilly in here."

I returned to my own bed and slept. I was going a little nuts.

Night arrived, but I couldn't sleep anymore. I drew pictures of Edgewood and I sculpting together. My arm in a sling, I had a tough time moving the charcoal pencils that had been placed beside my bed. Objects in my drawings appeared lopsided. Edgewood's nose was crooked, his head like a deflated beach ball. I looked like a melting snow sculpture of a person. Soon, fresh morning air carried the chirps of birds through my window.

My dad tapped me on the shoulder.

"What?" I said, blinking.

"You've been released," he said.

We drove home in his car.

After a day of recovery, my dad convinced me to complete my last week at the mill.

I spent hours simply walking around the plant, watching men blast away Edgewood's final murals and graffiti art with pressure washers. Greens and blues trickle. A stream of rainbow sludge ran from the rolling mill to a drain near a back parking lot. My dad's office remained freckled with paint from the day Edgewood and I vandalized the walls. He polished a new hunk of steel as he watched the pressure-washers carry out his orders.

OUTSIDE MY BEDROOM, I found three hundred dollars tacked to the door. My dad must've left it here, hoping to pay his way through an apology. Before thinking through the consequences of my actions, I tore one of the bills in half, to see how it felt. Tearing was difficult with the broken muscles in my shoulder. The money made such a small sound. A hundred dollars should've made more noise than a twenty, I thought. To experiment, I pulled out a one and tore it length-wise. My head bent toward the sound.

No, the same.

Three hundred dollars torn to confetti, I left it in an envelope tacked to my dad's door.

A long afternoon drive came to an end at the café. I dropped in to drug myself with coffee and see how many of my drawings had sold. The girl at the counter told me that customers had bought them all. "You ought to draw some more of them things," she said. "You'd make a nice living."

"Actually, you might be interested in some sketches of my mom. I draw so much these days I have plenty to spare. Funny, a few weeks ago I was completely blocked."

The night before I'd imagined my mom in an open casket at her funeral, and I'd drawn dozen versions of her corpse. I showed them to my admirer and she said, "Honey, you been okay lately?"

"Why do you say that?" My lips quivered. "You don't like my latest work?"

"It's just that, well, your mama ain't got a mouth."

Back at the house, I found my dad at the kitchen table. He sat hunched over a microscope. From the front door, he looked as if he might be on the verge of an historical discovery in metallurgical engineering. His fingers adjusted the knobs on each side of the device, bringing a tiny shred of paper in and out of focus. Then I realized his purpose: he was trying to salvage the money I'd torn to pieces and tacked to his door. As I approached I remembered this microscope from a home science kit he'd bought more than a decade ago, for my fourth birthday. My admiration diminished. With every step my dad became less a scientist, more a kindergartener. My dad, a man of nearly fifty years, had decided to use my old science kit to pass his afternoon. I sneezed, but he barely flinched. He simply pressed his eye sockets harder against the binocular lenses and arranged a few flakes of cash with tweezers. They were awkward plastic tweezers, yellow and thick, which had come with the kit.

I stood behind him, trying to understand his madness. A magnifying glass also lay on the table, beside an ashtray piled with freshly smoked cigarettes. Beneath his magnifying glass lay one partially reconstructed face of President Someone.

For some reason, I didn't feel quite myself. I wanted to apologize and beg forgiveness for what I'd done to his hard-earned money. Now that I watched my dad's painstaking care, the way his hands trembled just slightly as he reached for another green flake with his tweezers, I couldn't even remember why I'd torn apart the money. Instead of apologizing, a jesting spirit took possession of me. "That looks fantastic," I laughed and clapped. "Who would've thought you'd have the patience, you know, to sit there for hours and hours and rebuild all that money? Wait, you're Mister Persistence. I'm so proud of you these days."

I must've been possessed by my mom's ghost.

My dad placed his tweezers on the table. "Sarah?"

"That's my name. Say it three times and I'll grant you a wish."

"Maybe you should sit down," he said. "When's the last time you slept?"

"Congratulations. You were the first to find out." My palms slapped the table and I did a cheer. "I haven't slept at all, at least not to my knowledge!"

My dad looked concerned. The old wrinkles and worry lines in his face reactivated, bringing back memories of dear old mom's psychotic episodes. "Have you eaten?" he asked.

"Oh, what is food, really? I'm on a seafood diet. See food, don't eat it. Dad, now I have a serious question. Where is the whiskey?"

"You know where the whiskey is," he said. "But I'd recommend you eat first."

"And what have you done about Edgewood's funeral? I want him to have the best one ever. We need balloons, obviously, and let's hire a violinist. And I want him buried seven feet under, not six like everybody else."

"Sarah, why did you tear up all of this money?"

"Oh, that money? Well, your birthday's coming up and I wanted to get you a great puzzle. Can't do much better than that. You'll be busy for hours and hours, and do you know what else? I'm thinking we should do karaoke."

His head rattled. "What are you talking about?"

"At Edgewood's funeral." I snapped my fingers in his face. "Jeez, kid. Are you awake?"

PLANNING TO MOVE INTO EDGEWOOD'S PRISON for the wilting days of summer, I packed up all of my stuff except for my mom's paintings, which seemed to chant, "Leave us alone." All right, already! I emptied my room of possessions—sketchpad, books, a dirty plate—then I backed out, closing the door as if I were sealing the entrance to some Mesopotamian queen's burial chamber. I hauled ass over to the prison. It was going to be like camping, great fun. My blood ran laps through my veins and arteries. I kept having to tell my organs to slow down.

Before heading out, I scanned my old room for any stragglers—a sock, a little stick of charcoal. Nope, all empty! The last thing I saw was a single string of light tied from the blinds to a painting, one drowning mill worker's finger illuminated, the rest of her paintings a dull gray, like sheets of paper erased to death.

At Edgewood's, I lay in a cage on the first floor. I wasn't asleep exactly. All I could do was stare into the ceiling and tingle with plans.

I had a week left in Columbia, and I had so much to do. I had to plan Edgewood's funeral, and I had to paint, of course. I just stared and stared, hoping the angry mobs in Edgewood's murals would tear me apart.

In six days I would host a funeral ten times better than the one my dad had planned for my mom. Feeling guilty about many things, I imagine, my dad gave me a credit card and said to do what I thought best. I toured a dozen mortuaries and funeral homes.

My first stop of the day was a place called Marvin's Funeral Garden. A bald man with a Santa beard named Marvin Jr. showed me a video on planning with a budget. He jammed the video into a dusty VCR and coughed, unfolding chairs for us. The screen faded in and an announcer's voice boomed from the speakers. It was the bald man, Marvin Jr. He pranced through his own funeral home like a car salesman, pointing at yellow signs with fake cobwebs flung on to them. "Dying is just so expensive these days," Marvin said, "most people can't even afford to do it anymore!" His eyes and mouth popped open in one grim chuckle.

The screen cut to Marvin in his cemetery, tossing dollars down a freshly dug plot. "Some bastards'll charge you as much as ten grand for a funeral these days. They lay guilt trips on us if we hunt for bargains." Marvin tossed a handful of cash down the plot and waved at it. The camera zoomed in as he proclaimed, "But getting fleeced don't honor dear old Dad, does it?"

Marvin began to march before a cheap montage of video clips from tourist hotspots around the country and beyond. "Georgia, Tennessee, Florida, Mississippi, France, Ecuador, French Guiana, Mars, the Sun. We don't give a rat's behind where you live or where they died." A camera trick popped him into a dungeon where he slipped his arm around a skeleton. "Miss Daisy, you can bury your old hubby with dignity for the special low price of four-ninety-nine ninety five. All you need is flexible standards and a little creativity."

As soon as the video ended, I grabbed my bag and told Marvin I'd think about it. He handed me his business card, which looked like something you'd hand out as a gag at Halloween parties. His business logo was printed in red Gothic font on front and back, a black widow hanging from the end of his name by a thread of web. Tombstones bracketed his phone number at the bottom.

"By the way, babe. That's my personal number, too, just in case you want to go out for a drink or two and talk about your recent loss. Know what I mean?"

"That's so sweet, thanks."

"How about a goodbye kiss? Hey, I might die tomorrow. Live for today, that's what I say."

"No, I really have to run now. I admire your style. Bye."

In the end, I decided to go with Hawthorne & Sons, a place downtown that ran a smooth operation despite the strange name. They showed me picture books of past funerals and then guided me through a bewildering selection of caskets. I was ready to dump money like a bad boyfriend, but even the managers urged me to rent a display coffin if Edgewood was headed to the crematorium. They sold me on their deluxe package, which meant they did everything. "What kind of catering?" I asked.

"Simple's usually best," one man said.

"Not when it comes to my Edgewood. We need dazzle. Can you do . . . " I snapped my fingers, trying to think. "How about some shrimp cocktails, and I want fancy drinks. A wine and whiskey bar would be very nice. Oh, oh! And balloons!"

"With all due respect," a woman said. "I'm not sure the guests will see that in good taste."

"Do you guys charge a gratuity?"

They scoffed, but in the end I prevailed. After all, I was the one dressed in black for a reason.

I wanted to send out embossed invitations. But because of time constraints, I simply sent out a mass email that read, "You are cordially invited to attend Edgewood Crake's funeral this Friday. Event will commence at noon sharp at Hawthorne & Sons. Gourmet food to be served. Please RSVP Sarah West at phone number below." I invited everyone I knew, including all the steel mill crews.

The corpse doll I'd dug up two months ago became my new best friend. At night I sometimes cradled her, rocked her to sleep, sang to her. I enjoyed combing the doll's hair with a needle. I even leaned into mirrors for hours, just studying the similarities between our faces. Her deep blue eyelids and mine, the deep gray crescents under her eyes and mine. Her purple lips and mine. Her ashtray skin and mine. I began to wonder if she felt pain and, if not, whether I could feel her pain for her. Driving my needle into her forehead one midnight, I waited for the sting to touch my brow. Nothing happened. I tried again. I stabbed and stabbed. Nothing. Slowly as the sun inched upwards and the sky blued I grew angry with my doll and myself, both impervious to voodoo. I looked up spells on the Internet, but they all failed. Finally I sealed the doll inside her miniature coffin and dug a deep hole beneath an oak tree in someone's backyard. Following the burial, I snapped out of my disturbing trance and wondered when this awful metamorphosis would complete.

Later that morning, as I readied for the drive to work, I saw my corpse doll returned from the grave. I had climbed in the driver's seat and was just about to twist the keys, when a Labrador pranced by, dead doll in his teeth, and dropped her lifeless body on the brick steps of my portico. I chuckled at the sight of it and then fell asleep on my steering wheel. When I awoke, some wild creatures had torn her apart, leaving only a head and a chewed torso. I drove to the plant, refreshed and ready for more funeral planning.

DURING THE FINAL PHASE of the funeral bash, not one single member of Edgewood's family called. I remembered one or two vague comments about a falling out with his parents, and yet I could only guess why they didn't want to come. Maybe Edgewood wouldn't even want them at his burial, their cool eyes judging the corpse against his image in their memories. My dad said he had no contact information for those folks anyway, so I decided the loss was theirs.

The big day finally came. That morning at Hawthorne & Sons, I hung black and blue balloons in bunches of ten. The caterers arrived and asked if they had the right address. They'd never served a funeral before. I told them, "Yes, sir. Come on in."

They unfolded tables and draped cloth and uncovered the trays. Lobster, shrimp, seven cheeses. They arranged the plastic snifters, and I popped the champagne.

Mill workers arrived in pairs and quartets, followed by the Elvis-white casket that held my dear Edge.

Caterers rolled in another casket filled with dry ice, all according to my directions. I flipped open the lid and started plunging in sodas so they'd be death cold after the service. After that I began to arrange the guest gifts, which I'd made myself: Edgewood dolls. I had painted the skin cornflower blue, the lips maroon. Everyone would have one to take home.

Edgewood's steel buddies packed the pews. They chatted and sipped and popped shrimp. Meanwhile, I clicked open the casket and, to my shock, found something had gone terribly wrong.

I swung around and glared at the pair of representatives from the funeral home who'd delivered him. "What the hell is this?" I said, pointing at the body. "This coat is navy blue." I slammed my feet on the hardwood floor. "I said turquoise, to match his eyes. Turquoise! I'll fix this myself. Wheel him into the back." Noticing about a dozen oval-mouthed attendants, I pointed at one wearing the color coat I wanted. "That's perfect. Sir, can we borrow your jacket?"

Any sane person would've been terrified into submission. But I offered him five hundred dollars cash, and he nodded. He followed me into a back room. I directed the funeral home goons to lift Edgewood up, just high enough to replace the jacket. When I got the new jacket on and buttoned the buttons, I gave Edgewood a final hug and lay him back to rest. I whispered in his ear, "There you go, sugar. I know you like turquoise better. Don't you?"

I tickled Edgewood's chin.

A grandfather clock chimed the hour. Noon.

Time to fire up this party.

"Ladies and gentlemen," I said, when the clock hands met on twelve. I placed my special surprise box on top of the casket, a snow white box with a red bow. "We're gathered here today to unite this man and this woman in holy matrimony." I spoke with sly hand gestures to indicate the parties involved: Me and my beloved. "If anyone has a problem, speak now or forever hold your peace."

Silence. A sea of shoulders rolled in discomfort.

"Wonderful. And so now I'll present the rings."

I pulled off the top of my surprise box. A mannequin hand sprung up. On the tip of the index finger were two simple gold rings. One had been my mom's engagement ring, the other my dad's. He'd left it on the nightstand when he moved to Columbia. My mom had saved it, worn both.

I practically had to screw the ring onto Edgewood's finger.

"Do you take this man to be your lawfully wedded husband," I said, "to have and to hold. Till death do you part?"

Gasps.

"I do," I said, and then I turned to Edgewood. "Do you take this woman to be your lawfully wedded wife, to have and to hold. Till death do you part?"

My dad rose from the center of the audience. He edged his way into the aisle.

"I do," I said. "Dad, stop. You had your chance to object. Stop."

He continued in wide strides

"You may kiss the bride," I shouted, but before I could my dad had me in his arms. He wanted that kiss all for himself.

"Stop," I said. "You're ruining my wedding!"

His employees surrounded us, their funeral attire blinding me in black. Watching them encircle us, I thought of crows diving down on a helpless dove. I kept shouting that they were spoiling everything. Not until the casket closed on Edgewood did I lose it, eyes tearing and everything. My dad held me back. The casket sailed off, carried by impromptu pall bearers. I was still surrounded by black. I couldn't tell funeral clothes from the general darkness that was falling on me, like curtains at the end of a performance. Everything in me sagged, my muscles, my thoughts, my eyes. I wanted to go home.

15

DARTMOUTH. That's where I would find Orozco's masterpiece, *The Epic of American Civilization*, unfolding across the walls of a college library. At a gas station I bought a map and spread it across the floor of one of Edgewood's jail cells, where I red-inked a route from South Carolina to New England. Dartmouth. The name echoed in my head. That's where I could release Edgewood, one handful at a time.

On the prison steps I enjoyed a strengthening breeze that blew through my hair and made me sway like a tree. For practice I dipped my hand into the coffee can and tossed. As it scattered I tried to count the grains and guessed what part of Edgewood those ashes had come from.

I sleep-walked into the prison and draped myself on a chair, wondering what to do with Edgewood's books and a small city of paint supplies. I didn't even know what to do with the murals, pressure wash them? Photograph them and spend a lifetime developing Edgewood's posthumous career?

Night came on quickly, as if the sun were fainting. I chose to sleep in the same room as *Cobbled*.

The naked floor was cold.

The third Friday of August would've been my last day at work. My dad might've treated me to a farewell lunch, but I still wasn't hungry. I knew people were staring at me wherever I went. I must've looked like one of Giacometti's last sculptures.

The highway was like a big dead tree, branches everywhere, and I was one of hundreds of ants following a trail to some rotting piece of flesh.

I followed I-95 up the East Coast, watching the cars, pleased with the way the darkness brought out the red in their eyes.

I played a game reading license plates, wondering where people were headed, based on their home states. Trucks merged and peeled off the right lane. I wondered what they carried.

With one, I didn't have to guess. A sixteen-wheeler rolled into my lane, ahead of me. I braked to accommodate. A logo on the back implied steel mill, and it was carrying scrap inside a rickety side kit. The plywood boards bulged against the flimsy steel standards.

I called my dad, who answered on one ring like always. "It's me," I said. "I'm behind a scrap truck, ironically. I wanted to call and let you know I'm not going to be home this weekend. I'm taking a trip."

"Not a good place to be, behind one of those," he said. His voice was very calm. "Try moving over."

No, I wanted to say. It was fate. If something fell off the back, who was to say?

"I just wanted to let you know. I'm going to spend the weekend in Dartmouth. Sightseeing, a little vacation before school."

"You might not be going to school if you don't change lanes. Please. It's likely, far more likely than you realize. It's easy. Or slow down and give it some distance. These things, you don't know."

"I do. And when I can change lanes maybe I will. It's okay, Dad. No stress. Sorry I went nuts last week. It's pretty much gone now."

He sighed. "I guess a lot has happened this summer, not much of it great. But I've done my best. What can I say to get you to come back? You need rest. Now's not a good time to be traveling up to wherever. It sounds far. You're in no shape to be behind a wheel. I'm serious. Name it, whatever you want."

"You can't buy people."

"But you don't have anything without money, not even people."

"Ah, true. I guess I should get back to the road."

"Hold on a minute, Sarah. You know I pieced together that money you tore up. The bank was even about to accept it."

"Like I said, sorry. Glad I didn't ruin your budget."

"But I changed my mind."

"I'm glad you managed to fix another problem. That's your business, after all."

"Are you listening, Sarah? I changed my mind. I didn't deposit the money."

"Well, so what? I mean fuck. Cash, check, credit card. I'm sick of hearing about money."

Sirens appeared on the horizon of the opposite side of the highway. Cars slowed and formed a chain of rubberneckers. The truck in front of me braked. A piece of scrap tumbled along the top of the mountain of steel.

"Shit," I said.

"I burned the money. I used it to start a fire is what I'm saying. It's gone. What's going on? A wreck?"

The chewed blob of steel rolled over the edge of the side kit and dangled. The truck and I picked up a little speed just after passing an ambulance and two highway patrol cars. No bodies that I could tell, just a sprattle of glass and dented aluminum. A Ford Explorer's hood had crumpled like messy bed sheets.

"Dad, thanks. I didn't think you'd do that. All the stories Mom told."

"I did, and after I'd stayed up all night for the better part of this week. I kept asking myself why. Burning all three hundred bucks felt right, like I was going along with you. Doing things the way you wanted. Anyway, the fire's still going," he joked. "Maybe it'll be here when you get back."

"I'd hope so," I said. "You paid enough for it."

We laughed.

Since when had we laughed at the same time?

"I have to pull off and call the highway patrol," I said. "This scrap truck's in bad shape."

"You work too much," he said. "I'd feel better if you came home. But I guess it's up to you. Be safe."

After calling the highway patrol, I couldn't get used to the silence again. The silence was like a medicine or a drug, or an addiction. My hips ached, and so did my shoulder. My eyes felt like they'd sink down into my brain if I kept driving. I had to stop.

I cruised down an exit into a budget hotel, nothing shocking one way or the other. The desk clerk offered me an extra roll of toilet paper because I resembled his daughter who'd disappeared five years ago. The stairs to my room smelled like dead flowers. When I opened the door, a painting of crows greeted me, gunmetal eyes and black beaks. Although these birds couldn't hurt me, I lifted them off their hooks anyway and hid them under the bed. Even then, I could fool myself into hearing them caw.

MR. ANJALU, OF ALL PEOPLE, bought my mom's house. I had to admit: the thought of my old art teacher curled up in her bed, his wine in her fridge, made me smirk. After signing the final papers, he hired me to help unpack and hang his artwork. Mr. Anjalu's furniture puzzled me. His couch looked like one of a dozen Giacometti sculptures welded together and coated with a thin skin of leather. I couldn't imagine sitting on it for long, but he explained that he'd pleasured at least a dozen women on this contraption. The loveseat, as well as another seven or eight home furnishings, seemed to have been inspired by the movie *Metropolis*. You had to climb into the seat on a ladder with circular rungs.

"What in the world is this one for?" I said, wheeling a slim cage in on a hand truck.

Mr. Anjalu held open the front door. "That is for none of your corporation, little one. I mean for none of your industry, or firm."

"You mean none of my *business*?"

"Yes, you know what I mean."

His bed consisted of two steel pillars and a bundle of wires and hooks. We strung his contraption together in my mom's old bedroom. Once finished, I asked Mr. Anjalu to demonstrate how to sleep in this mess of metal. He strung together a kind of spider web from the cables. Then he strapped himself into this trap by the wrists, ankles, neck, and waist. He hung between the steel towers, topsy turvy, so that his eyeglasses dangled from his ears as he faced the floor. "Ah," he sighed. "I could fall into nap any minute."

Mr. Anjalu unloaded his paintings. I hung some of my favorites in the upstairs hallway. In these he had gone beyond Pollack. Stars dotted canvases he'd painted a thick, textured black. Pairs of some specs behaved like eyes, coordinated, curious, perhaps dangerous. One painting reminded me of outer space, another a dense forest full of owls and bats and wolves—all staring at me.

We unpacked his books in the living room, where boxes made a skyline of cardboard.

"It is sad very much that I did not get your news before funeral," he said, cutting open a box. Foam peanuts bloomed through the opening. "How your summer has been, aside from many deaths?"

"Not bad, I guess. What doesn't kill you just makes things harder."

"Tell your sorrows to the singers in church, the chorus. You know what I mean." Mr. Anjalu's hands ploughed the peanuts, and they gushed out, as if the box were frothing. "I draw her a few times, by the way, before she went terrible in her head. You know what I mean."

"Yeah, I do."

He tugged a few cases of videos from the field of foam, mostly artist documentaries, and read them silently while reminiscing. "You and your mother, rest her brain or spirit or what have you, was so very beautiful. Always. I like the painting of beautiful talented women." Suddenly, he snapped his fingers. "You know, little one. These paintings, I have them. They are in the trunk. Let me go get."

He returned with two oil paintings and a charcoal sketch. She hugged knees in one, a body of empty air in the other. In all three she never smiled, but I could tell she was happy. "Take them," he said.

I agreed.

"And now I must speak to you with Edwardness," Mr. Anjalu said. "I mean Albertness. Frankness, you know what I mean." He climbed the ladder to his loveseat and removed his eyeglasses, burning me through with his eyes, which were blackened by insomnia. I'd never seen Mr. Anjalu without his eyeglasses until now.

"Speak to me frankly about what?" I asked.

"Little one, you have finally started to make art again. Yes?"

"That's right," I said. "I had a tough summer."

"Buffalo shit, little one. You get, what would you say, sorry for yourself. I think, yes, very sorry. Very sad about mother, right?"

I nodded again.

"Well, don't be. She was good artist. But not very subtle. You are better."

I blinked.

Mr. Anjalu ran a finger along his chin. "I can tell all about you, just by body movement. The way you look at mother's paintings. You think she does better than you. But you are ready for what I think?"

I numbed from the neck down. Unable to move, I pointed my eyes at a corner. "Tell me," I said.

"So foolish to keep mourning this person. Her car accident become good thing for you. No longer waiting for her approval."

"How do you know?"

"I will see new work you do. Give to me for critique. Why not put in for show, gallery?"

"So it's okay to seek approval from you?"

Mr. Anjalu adjusted his glasses. "My approval means different. You know this."

"Like where would I display my work?" I asked. "Other than some stupid coffee shop."

"Like my gallery you display it," he said and clapped his hands, then rubbed them together. "I open one soon, right downtown near the Ivory. The Emerald. You know what I mean."

"Emory?" I said.

"You know, yes. That is the place."

My head shook. "Really?"

"You will submit work for opening show, little one. Or I will come hunt you down. You know what I mean?"

"Okay."

"And in the just case," he said. "You have sketchbook with you?"

I'd left it atop a box. I handed him the whole of my summer's work since July. He thumbed through, making pleasant guttural sounds. "Yes, I will keep and choose which to frame and show." He shrugged then, sliding my book under one arm. "Besides, I am similar story. Very sad in the childhood. You know what I mean. I watch my own mother get her body blown up in distant country. She went boom, boom, and more boom, and we could not find body to bury. I am six when happens. No, five and three-quarters. Besides, having crazy person always bothering you, what nuisance! Be glad for yourself. Now you focus on work that is yours."

"Gotcha," I mouthed.

"And for your boyfriend, he was good as well. Sad for him to die. He had good idea, to paint steel industry. But you know he spend too many years there. He become coward. Not like you. You aren't coward. You are second bravest person I ever meet." He sighed and rubbed his knees. "And now you will hate me for many days, I know. But this I say out of respect. Thank you for helping to move. Now, bye-bye."

I stood. "I don't hate you," I whispered. Then I walked out of Mr. Anjalu's house, wondering why I felt so good.

My dad and I planned a helicopter ride over the plant for my last morning of summer, when I would spill the rest of Edgewood's ashes into the breeze. The night before our scheduled flight, however, I made a terrible mistake and placed the urn beside my makeshift bed for company. I'd chosen to spend my final night in Columbia in Edgewood's prison studio, which was now emptied of his belongings and hollow as a cave. After midnight I rose from the grave of sleep to investigate a noise and tripped. My foot kicked the urn across the moonlit room. The urn bounced off the wall and scattered Edgewood's remains all over the prison floor. For two hours I tried to sweep this fine powder into a mound with my hands. Then

I gave up. I realized that these gray granules were ashes, just ashes, nothing more. Why spread them? Why not leave them here, where they belonged?

I turned the urn upside down and dumped out the rest of my former beloved, then pitched the urn into a barred prison window. The ceramic clapped against the iron. Pieces exploded everywhere. One of them embedded into a knuckle on my right fist. Another sliver I stepped on and sliced the big toe on my left foot. I cursed, calmed myself, licked my palms clean, and almost slept. At some point in the night, my wounds clotted.

At sunrise, I made a pilgrimage to the mill and watched the first thunderstorm we'd had in months. Wind toyed with a streetlight up the road. The mill's parking lot steamed. Trees swayed like the insane. In the fog, I struggled to see any part of myself, even my hands. As vapor enveloped me, I groped my way to the guard shack and sat just before the gate. I drew blind, relying on a picture of scrap heaps, trains, and steel on the insides of my eyes. I could've been sitting in heaven, which might not be such a cheery place after all, full of winged ghosts who sit on clouds, like the homeless on benches, wishing they could descend. I felt the warm cotton of the air, the charcoal at my fingertips, and nothing else.

Acknowledgements

THANKS TO EVERYONE at CMC Steel for going easy, but not too easy, on the summer help. Thanks also go to family, friends, and workshop partners David Axe and Sara Saylor for many fine hours spent at Cool Beans and Adriana's. This book and my writing in general grew with the help and support of faculty at the University of South Carolina—especially Donald Greiner, Matthew J. Bruccoli, Ben Greer, David Cowart, Janette Turner Hospital, Elise Blackwell, and Fred Dings. I'm also indebted to the S.C. Arts Commission, the S.C. State Library, the Humanities Council SC, and Hub City Writers Project, as well as Michael Curtis and Percival Everett, for enabling this novel's publication and ensuring its quality.

THE HUB CITY WRITERS PROJECT is a non-profit organization whose mission is to foster a sense of community through the literary arts. We do this by publishing books from and about our community; encouraging, mentoring, and advancing the careers of local writers; and seeking to make Spartanburg a center for the literary arts.

Our metaphor of organization purposefully looks backward to the nineteenth century when Spartanburg was known as the "hub city," a place where railroads converged and departed. At the beginning of the twenty-first century, Spartanburg has become a literary hub of South Carolina with an active and nationally celebrated core group of poets, fiction writers, and essayists. We celebrate these writers—and the ones not yet discovered—as one of our community's greatest assets. William R. Ferris, former director of the Center for Southern Studies, says of the emerging South, "Our culture is our greatest resource. We can shape an economic base . . . And it won't be an investment that will disappear."

HUB CITY WRITERS PROJECT TITLES

Hub City Anthology • John Lane & Betsy Wakefield Teter, editors

Hub City Music Makers • Peter Cooper

Hub City Christmas • John Lane & Betsy Wakefield Teter, editors

New Southern Harmonies • Rosa Shand, Scott Gould, Deno Trakas, George Singleton

The Best of Radio Free Bubba • Meg Barnhouse, Pate Jobe, Kim Taylor, Gary Phillips

Family Trees: The Peach Culture of the Piedmont • Mike Corbin

Seeing Spartanburg: A History in Images • Philip Racine

The Seasons of Harold Hatcher • Mike Hembree

The Lawson's Fork: Headwaters to Confluence • David Taylor, Gary Henderson

Hub City Anthology 2 • Betsy Wakefield Teter, editor

Inheritance • Janette Turner Hospital, editor

In Morgan's Shadow • A Hub City Murder Mystery

A Note on the Type

THE TEXT OF THIS BOOK is set in Arno Pro, named after the river that runs through Florence. Created by Adobe principal designer Robert Slimbach, the meticulously crafted typeface draws on the warmth and readability of early humanist types of the fifteenth and sixteenth centuries.

While inspired by classic Venetian tradition, the sturdy Arno is distinctly contemporary. Pages set in the face result in strong text color reminiscent of books set in metal foundry type.

Printed in the United States
214057BV00001B/22/P

9 781891 885662